BRENT LIBRARIES

Please return/renew this item
by the last date shown.
Books may also be renewed by
phone or online.
Tel: 0333 370 4700
On-line www.brent.gov.uk/libraryservice

EX LIBRIS

VINTAGE CLASSICS

A Scandinavian Christmas

Festive Tales for a Nordic Noël

VINTAGE

1 3 5 7 9 10 8 6 4 2

Vintage Classics is part of the Penguin Random House
group of companies whose addresses can be found at global.
penguinrandomhouse.com

Penguin
Random House
UK

First published in the United States as *A Very Scandinavian Christmas*
by New Vessel Press in 2019

First published in Great Britain by Vintage Classics in 2021

penguin.co.uk/vintage-classics

A CIP catalogue record for this book is available from
the British Library

ISBN 9781784877675

Typeset in 12/15 pt Bembo Std
by Integra Software Services Pvt. Ltd, Pondicherry

Printed and bound in Great Britain by Clays Ltd, Elcograf S.p.A.

The authorised representative in the EEA is Penguin Random House
Ireland, Morrison Chambers, 32 Nassau Street, Dublin D02 YH68.

Penguin Random House is committed to a sustainable future for
our business, our readers and our planet. This book is made from
Forest Stewardship Council® certified paper.

Contents

CONTENTS

A SCANDINAVIAN CHRISTMAS

A CHRISTMAS GUEST

Selma Lagerlöf

One of those who had lived the life of a pensioner at Ekeby was little Ruster, who could transpose music and play the flute. He was of low origin and poor, without home and without relations. Hard times came to him when the company of pensioners were dispersed.

He then had no horse or cariole, no fur coat nor red-painted luncheon basket. He had to go on foot from house to house and carry his belongings tied in a blue striped cotton handkerchief. He buttoned his coat all the way up to his chin, so that no one should need to know in what condition his shirt and waistcoat were, and in its deep pockets he kept his most precious possessions: his flute taken to pieces, his flat brandy bottle and his music pen.

His profession was to copy music, and if it had been as in the old days, there would have been no lack of work for him. But with every passing year music was less prac-ticed in Värmland. The guitar, with its mouldy, silken ribbon and its worn screws, and the dented horn, with faded tassels and cord, were put away in the lumber room in the attic, and the dust settled inches deep on the long, iron-bound violin boxes. Yet the less little Ruster had to do with flute and music pen, so much the more must he turn to the brandy flask, and at last he became quite a drunkard. It was a great pity.

He was still received at the manor houses as an old friend, but there were complaints when he came and joy when he went. There was an odour of dirt and brandy about him, and if he had only a couple of glasses of wine or one toddy, he grew confused and told unpleasant stories. He was the torment of the hospitable houses.

One Christmas he came to Löfdala, where Liljekrona, the great violinist, had his home. Liljekrona had also been one of the pensioners of Ekeby, but after the death of the major's wife, he returned to his quiet farm and remained there. Ruster came to him a few days before Christmas, in the midst of all the preparations, and asked for work. Liljekrona gave him a little copying to keep him busy.

'You ought to have let him go immediately,' said his wife, 'now he will certainly take so long with that that we will be obliged to keep him over Christmas.'

'He must be somewhere,' answered Liljekrona.

And he offered Ruster toddy and brandy, sat with him, and lived over again with him the whole Ekeby time. But he was out of spirits and disgusted by him, like everyone else, although he would not let it be seen, for old friendship and hospitality were sacred to him.

In Liljekrona's house for three weeks now they had been preparing to receive Christmas. They had been living in discomfort and bustle, had sat up with diplights and torches till their eyes grew red, had been frozen in the outhouse with the salting of meat and in the brew house with the brewing of the beer. But both the mistress and the servants gave themselves up to it all without grumbling.

When all the preparations were done and the holy evening came, a sweet enchantment would sink down over them. Christmas would loosen all tongues, so that jokes and jests, rhymes and merriment would flow of themselves without effort. Everyone's feet would wish to twirl in the dance, and from memory's dark corners words and melodies would rise, although no one could believe that they were there. And then everyone was so good, so good!

Now when Ruster came the whole household at Löfdala thought that Christmas was spoiled. The mistress and the older children and the old servants were all of the same opinion. Ruster caused them a suffocating disgust. They were moreover afraid that when he and Liljekrona began to rake up the old memories, the artist's blood would flame up in the great violinist and his home would lose him. Formerly he had not been able to remain long at home.

No one can describe how they loved their master on the farm, since they had had him with them a couple of years. And what he had to give! How much he was to his home, especially at Christmas! He did not take his place on any sofa or rocking stool, but on a high narrow wooden bench in the corner of the fireplace. When he was settled there he started off on adventures. He traveled about the Earth, climbed up to the stars, and even higher. He played and talked by turns, and the whole household gathered about him and listened. Life grew proud and beautiful when the richness of that one soul shone on it.

Therefore they loved him as they loved Christmastime, pleasure, the spring sun. And when little Ruster came, their Christmas peace was destroyed. They had worked in vain if he was coming to tempt away their master. It was unjust that the drunkard should sit at the Christmas table in a happy house and spoil the Christmas pleasure.

On the forenoon of Christmas Eve little Ruster had his music written out, and he said something about going, although of course he meant to stay.

Liljekrona had been influenced by the general feeling, and therefore said quite lukewarmly and indifferently that Ruster had better stay where he was over Christmas.

Little Ruster was inflammable and proud. He twirled his moustache and shook back the black artist's hair that stood like a dark cloud over his head. What did Liljekrona mean? Should he stay because he had nowhere else to go? Oh, only think how they stood and waited for him in the big ironworks in the parish of Bro! The guest room was in order, the glass of welcome filled. He was in great haste. He only did not know to which he ought to go first.

'Very well,' answered Liljekrona, 'you may go if you will.'

After dinner little Ruster borrowed horse and sleigh, coat and furs. The stable boy from Löfdala was to take him to some place in Bro and drive quickly back, for it threatened snow.

No one believed that he was expected, or that there was a single place in the neighbourhood where he was welcome. But they were so anxious to be rid of him that they put the thought aside and let him depart. 'He wished it himself,' they said; and then they thought that now they would be glad.

But when they gathered in the dining room at five o'clock to drink tea and to dance around the Christmas tree, Liljekrona was silent and out of spirits. He did not

seat himself on the bench; he touched neither tea nor
punch; he could not remember any polka; the violin was
out of order. Those who could play and dance had to do
it without him.

Then his wife grew uneasy; the children were discontented, everything in the house went wrong. It was the
most lamentable Christmas Eve.

The porridge turned sour; the candles sputtered; the
wood smoked; the wind stirred up the snow and blew
bitter cold into the rooms. The stable boy who had driven
Ruster did not come home. The cook wept; the maids
scolded.

Finally Liljekrona remembered that no sheaves had
been put out for the sparrows, and he complained aloud
of all the women about him who abandoned old customs
and were newfangled and heartless. They understood
well enough that what tormented him was remorse that
he had let little Ruster go away from his home on
Christmas Eve.

After a while he went to his room, shut the door, and
began to play as he had not played since he had ceased
roaming. It was full of hate and scorn, full of longing and
revolt. 'You thought to bind me, but you must forge new
fetters. You thought to make me as small-minded as yourselves, but I turn to larger things, to the open. Commonplace

people, slaves of the home, hold me prisoner if it is in your power!'

When his wife heard the music, she said: 'Tomorrow he is gone, if God does not work a miracle in the night. Our inhospitableness has brought on just what we thought we could avoid.'

In the meantime little Ruster drove about in the snow-storm. He went from one house to the other and asked if there was any work for him to do, but he was not received anywhere. They did not even ask him to get out of the sledge. Some had their houses full of guests, others were going away on Christmas Day. 'Drive to the next neighbour,' they all said.

He could come and spoil the pleasure of an ordinary day, but not of Christmas Eve. Christmas Eve came but once a year, and the children had been rejoicing in the thought of it all the autumn. They could not put that man at a table where there were children. Formerly they had been glad to see him, but not since he had become a drunkard. Where should they put the fellow, moreover? The servants' room was too plain and the guest room too fine.

So little Ruster had to drive from house to house in the blinding snow. His wet moustache hung limply down over his mouth; his eyes were bloodshot and blurred, but the brandy was blown out of his brain. He began to wonder and to be amazed. Was it possible, was it possible that no one wished to receive him?

Then all at once he saw himself. He saw how miserable and degraded he was, and he understood that he was odious to people. 'It is the end of me,' he thought. 'No more copying of music, no more flute playing. No one on earth needs me; no one has compassion on me.'

The storm whirled and played, tore apart the drifts and piled them up again, took a pillar of snow in its arms and danced out into the plain, lifted one flake up to the clouds and chased another down into a ditch. 'It is so, it is so,' said little Ruster; 'while one dances and whirls it is play, but when one must be buried in the drift and forgotten, it is sorrow and grief.' But down they all have to go, and now it was his turn. To think that he had now come to the end!

He no longer asked where the man was driving him; he thought that he was driving in the land of death.

Little Ruster made no offerings to the gods that night. He did not curse flute playing or the life of a pensioner; he did not think that it had been better for him if he had ploughed the earth or sewn shoes. But he mourned that he was now a worn-out instrument, which pleasure could no longer use. He complained of no one, for he knew that when the horn is cracked and the guitar will not stay in tune, they must go. He became all at once a very humble man. He understood that it was the end of him, on this Christmas Eve. Hunger and cold would destroy him, for he understood nothing, was good for nothing, and had no friends.

The sledge stops, and suddenly it is light about him, and he hears friendly voices, and there is someone who is helping him into a warm room, and someone who is pouring warm tea into him. His coat is pulled off him, and several people cry that he is welcome, and warm hands rub life into his benumbed fingers.

He was so confused by it all that he did not come to his senses for nearly a quarter of an hour. He could not possibly comprehend that he had come back to Löfdala. He had not been at all conscious that the stable boy had grown tired of driving about in the storm and had turned home.

Nor did he understand why he was now so well received in Liljekrona's house. He could not know that Liljekrona's wife understood what a weary journey he had made that Christmas Eve, when he had been turned away from every door where he had knocked. She felt such compassion on him that she forgot her own troubles.

Liljekrona went on with the wild playing up in his room; he did not know that Ruster had come. The latter sat meanwhile in the dining room with the wife and the children. The servants, who used also to be there on Christmas Eve, had moved out into the kitchen away from their mistress's trouble.

The mistress of the house lost no time in setting Ruster to work. 'You hear, I suppose,' she said, 'that Liljekrona does nothing but play all the evening, and I must attend to setting the table and the food. The children are quite forsaken. You must look after these two smallest.'

Children were the kind of people with whom little Ruster had had least intercourse. He had met them neither in the bachelor's wing nor in the campaign tent, neither in wayside inns nor on the highways. He was almost shy of them, and did not know what he ought to say that was fine enough for them.

He took out his flute and taught them how to finger the stops and holes. There was one of four years and one of six. They had a lesson on the flute and were deeply interested in it. 'This is A,' he said, 'and this is C,' and then he blew the notes. Then the young people wished to know what kind of an A and C it was that was to be played.

Ruster took out his score and made a few notes.

'No,' they said, 'that is not right.' And they ran away for an *A B C* book.

Little Ruster began to hear their alphabet. They knew it and they did not know it. What they knew was not very much. Ruster grew eager; he lifted the little boys up, each on one of his knees, and began to teach them. Liljekrona's wife went out and in and listened quite in amazement. It sounded like a game, and the children were laughing the whole time, but they learned.

Ruster kept on for a while, but he was absent from what he was doing. He was turning over the old thoughts from out in the storm. It was good and pleasant, but nevertheless, it was the end of him. He was worn out. He ought to be thrown away. And all of a sudden he put his hands before his face and began to weep.

Liljekrona's wife came quickly up to him.

'Ruster,' she said, 'I can understand that you think that all is over for you. You cannot make a living with your music, and you are destroying yourself with brandy. But it is not the end, Ruster.'

'Yes,' sobbed the little flute player.

'Do you see that to sit as tonight with the children, that would be something for you? If you would teach children to read and write you would be welcomed everywhere. That is no less important an instrument on which to play, Ruster, than flute and violin. Look at them, Ruster!'

She placed the two children in front of him, and he looked up blinking as if he had looked at the sun. It seemed as if his little blurred eyes could not meet those of the children, which were big, clear, and innocent.

'Look at them, Ruster!' repeated Liljekrona's wife.

'I dare not,' said Ruster, for it was like a purgatory to look through the beautiful child eyes to the unspotted beauty of their souls.

Liljekrona's wife laughed loud and joyously.

'Then you must accustom yourself to them, Ruster. You can stay in my house as schoolmaster this year.'

Liljekrona heard his wife laugh and came out of his room. 'What is it?' he said. 'What is it?'

'Nothing,' she answered, 'but that Ruster has come again, and that I have engaged him as schoolmaster for our little boys.'

Liljekrona was quite amazed. 'Do you dare?' he said. 'Do you dare? Has he promised to give up – '

'No,' said the wife. 'Ruster has promised nothing. But there is much about which he must be careful when he has to look little children in the eyes every day. If it had not been Christmas, perhaps I would not have ventured; but when our Lord dared to place a little child who was his own son among us sinners, so can I also dare to let my little children try to save a human soul.'

Liljekrona could not speak, but every feature and wrinkle in his face twitched and twisted as always when he heard anything noble.

Then he kissed his wife's hand as gently as a child who asks for forgiveness and cried aloud: 'All the children must come and kiss their mother's hand.'

They did so, and then they had a happy Christmas in Liljekrona's house.

1910

A LEGEND OF MERCY

Zachris Topelius

* * * * *

On one side of the lake there was a large town; on the opposite shore stood a little lone cottage. The snow whirled over the frozen lake in great clouds and the wind was very keen; for it was winter and Christmastide in the world.

At the cottage there was poverty inside, but riches on the roof. Up there stood the great golden sheaf of grain about which the birds of heaven gathered joyfully for their Christmas feast, while inside the cottage food was scanty, as usual. The peasants' little children, however, listened happily to the birds' joyous twitter from the housetop, and took great delight in seeing the fine prints of the sparrow's tiny feet in the smooth snow roundabout.

'If we had threshed that grain instead of giving it to the sparrows, we might have had fresh wheaten rolls for the children for Christmas,' sighed the peasant's wife.

'Don't you know that the merciful are blessed?' asked the gentle old peasant with a kind glance at his dissatisfied wife.

'But to let the birds of the air eat our bread,' she sighed again.

'Yes, the birds. Furthermore, what matter, even if it were the wild beasts of the forest? Should we not show mercy? Besides, I have saved enough to be able to buy four fresh rolls and a can of milk for Christmas. Let us send the children across the lake to the town with their sled. They will easily get back with the things before evening.'

'But suppose they meet a wolf on the ice,' suggested the mother.

'I will give Arvid a big club,' said the father. 'He will get along all right, having that.'

So it happened that Arvid and his sister, Hanna, went to town to buy the treat of white rolls and milk. By this time the snow was piled in great drifts on the ice, and the children had difficulty in dragging the sled, so that when they turned toward home the early darkness was already beginning to settle down. They trudged through the snow as fast as they could, but the drifts were much higher than before, and darkness came on in earnest while they still had quite a long distance to go.

As they struggled on, something black moved in the darkness. When it came nearer, the children saw that it was a wolf.

'Don't be afraid, Hanna,' said Arvid. 'I have a good club.' And with these words, he raised it threateningly.

The wolf was now close beside the children but made no attempt to harm them. He only howled, but the howling was extraordinary for it sounded as if he uttered words in it – words that the children could understand. 'It is so cold, so cold,' howled the wolf. 'And my little ones have nothing to eat. Give me some bread for them in the name of mercy.'

'Poor little things!' said Hanna. 'We will give you *our* two rolls for them, and we ourselves will eat hard bread tonight, but father and mother must have their Christmas treat.'

'Many thanks,' said the wolf as he took the two fresh rolls and glided away.

The children strove on through deeper and deeper snow, but in a little while they heard some creature treading heavily behind them. It proved to be a bear.

The bear growled out something in his own language, and at first the children could not find out what he meant although they tried hard; but the bear kept on growling and finally, strangely enough, the children understood. The bear, too, desired a Christmas gift.

'It is so cold, so cold,' growled the big creature. 'All the water everywhere is frozen and my poor little ones have nothing to drink. Be merciful and give me a little milk for them.'

'How is this?' asked Arvid. 'Why are you not asleep in your den for the winter, as other bears are? But that is your affair. We will give you our half of the milk for your little ones. Hanna and I can very well drink water tonight, if only father and mother have something good for Christmas.'

'Many thanks,' said the bear, as he took the milk in a birch bark cone which he carried in his forepaws. Then with slow, pompous steps, he lumbered away into the darkness.

The children waded along through the drifts still more eagerly now, for they could see the Christmas lights shining through the windows of their home; but they had not gone far before an ugly owl came flapping along beside them.

'I will have bread and milk! I will have bread and milk!' screamed the owl, stretching out her long claws to scratch the children.

'Oh, ho!' said Arvid. 'If that is the kind you are, I shall have to teach you to be polite.' So saying, he gave the owl such a clever blow on the wings with his club that she flew screaming away.

Soon after this the children were at home, gaily beating the snow from their clothes in the little entry.

'We have met a wolf!' shouted Hanna.

'And given a bear some milk!' added Arvid.

'But the owl got a taste of the club!' laughed Hanna. Then they told all their adventures.

The parents looked thoughtfully at each other. How wonderful! To think that their children had shown mercy even to the wild beasts of the forest! What would happen next? What did it all mean?

It was now supper time. The peasant family gathered at the table upon which, besides the usual poor fare, was the half portion of the expected treat — all that the children had brought home.

Arvid and Hanna wished to eat only dry bread and drink only water, so that their parents might have the Christmas goodies; but the parents would not allow that. They joyfully shared with the children the two rolls and the half tankard of milk which were such luxuries.

But as they ate, they noticed something very marvelous. However often they broke and broke pieces from either of the rolls, the fresh, delicious, wheaten rolls never grew smaller; and however often they poured milk from the tankard into one bowl after another the milk never grew less!

While they were wondering greatly over this, they heard a scratching at the little window, and behold! There stood the wolf and the bear with their forepaws against the windowpane. Both animals grinned and nodded in a knowing, friendly way. An owl could be heard flapping behind them in the darkness, and calling out in a hoarse voice to Arvid:

'Sometimes hits
Sharpen wits.
Hoo, hoo! Hoo, hoo!
Not from need
But from greed
I begged of you.
Hoo, hoo! Hoo, hoo!'

Then her hoarse cries died away in the distance, and the two beasts, after a little more grinning and nodding, disappeared from the window.

The peasant and his wife and the children understood now that a blessing rested upon their Christmas food because it had been shared in mercy with those that needed it; and they finished their meal in wonder and thankfulness.

On Christmas morning when they went to get their breakfast of dry bread and water, not expecting to have anything else, they found to their amazement that both rolls and milk were as fresh as when the children bought them – and with no sign that the rolls had ever been broken or any milk used! And all that day it was the same! There were not only riches on the roof, but joy and plenty inside the peasants' cottage, where the children feasted and sang as gaily as did the sparrows, fluttering about their Christmas sheaf of golden grain.

1916

THE FUR COAT

Hjalmar Söderberg

It was a cold winter that year. People looked pinched and shrunken, except of course those who owned fur coats.

Justice Richardt had a monstrous fur coat. Indeed, it was quite in keeping with his position as director in a newly formed corporation. His old friend Dr. Henck, on the contrary, had no fur coat; but he had a beautiful wife and three children.

Dr. Henck was thin and pale; some people grow fat when they marry, others thin; Dr. Henck had grown thin.

It was Christmas Eve.

'I've had a pretty poor year this year,' said Dr. Henck to himself when, about three o'clock in the afternoon dusk, he was on his way to see his old friend John Richardt to borrow some money. 'Yes, I've had a very poor year.

My health is tottering – I might say ruined. On the other hand my patients have been remarkably well and need me seldom these days. I shall probably die soon; my wife thinks so too – I've seen that plainly enough; well, if it does come I wish it would be before the end of January when that damned life insurance premium is due.'

When he had reached this point in his thoughts he found himself at the corner of Regent and Halm streets. As he was crossing to go down Regent Street he slipped on the smooth sleigh track and tumbled down. At that moment a sleigh came by at full speed; the coachman swore and the horse turned instinctively to one side; nevertheless Dr. Henck's shoulder was struck by one of the runners and a screw or bolt caught in his coat and tore a big hole in one side.

People gathered about him. A policeman helped him to his feet; a young girl brushed the snow off him, and an old lady's gesticulations suggested that she would mend his torn coat if that were possible. A prince of the reigning house who happened to pass picked up the doctor's hat and placed it on his head and everything was all right again – everything but the coat.

'Good Lord, what's happened to you, Gustaf?' said Justice Richardt when Henck arrived at his office.

'I've been run over,' said Henck.

'That's just like you,' said Richardt laughing good-naturedly. 'You must put on my fur coat and I'll send a boy to my house for my overcoat.'

'Thanks,' said Dr. Henck.

And after he had borrowed the hundred crowns he needed he continued, 'Well, we'll expect you to dinner, of course.'

Richardt was a bachelor and it was his custom to spend Christmas Eve with the Hencks.

On his way home Henck was in better spirits than he had been for a long time.

'It's on account of the fur coat,' he told himself. 'If I had been clever I'd have got a fur coat long ago on credit. It would have strengthened me in my own esteem as well as raised me in the eyes of others. People are bound to pay more respect to a doctor in a fur coat than to one in an ordinary overcoat with frayed buttonholes; it's too bad that I didn't think of that before; it's too late now.'

He took a turn through King's Park. It was already dark and had started to snow again and the acquaintances he met did not recognise him.

'Who knows,' continued Henck to himself, 'perhaps it isn't too late. I'm not old yet and I may be mistaken about my health. I'm as poor as a fox in the woods but so was John Richardt not so very long ago. My wife has been cold and indifferent to me lately; perhaps she would care for me again if I could earn more money – and if I were dressed in a fur coat. It has occurred to me that she likes John more since he has owned a fur coat. She was quite taken with him as a young girl, but he never courted her. He used to say to her and to everyone that he would never dare marry on less than ten thousand a year – but I dared!

'Ellen was a poor girl and glad to be married. I don't think she was deeply in love with me, but I'm sure she cared for me during the first years of our marriage – one is never mistaken in such matters. Why shouldn't she care for me again then? When we were first married, she used to say mean little things to John whenever they met but then when he formed this corporation and took us to the theatre and bought a fur coat, of course she grew tired of being hateful to him as time went on.'

Henck had a few errands to do before dinner.

It was half past five when he reached home laden with packages. His left shoulder was very lame, but otherwise there was nothing that reminded him of the accident – except the fur coat.

'It'll be fun to see my wife's expression when she sees me in a fur coat,' said Henck to himself. The hall was dark, as the lamp was never lighted until dinner time.

'I hear her in the sitting room; she trips as lightly as a little bird,' thought Dr. Henck. 'It's strange how my heart warms whenever I hear her step in the next room.'

Dr. Henck was right when he thought his wife would give him a more loving greeting when he was dressed in a fur coat than she did ordinarily.

She nestled close to him in the darkest corner of the hall and put her arms around his neck and kissed him warmly. Then she buried her face in his collar and whispered, 'Gustaf isn't at home.'

'Yes,' answered Dr. Henck in a somewhat fluttering voice while he stroked her hair with both hands. 'Yes, he is at home.'

A cheerful fire crackled in Dr. Henck's library. On the table stood whiskey and water. Justice Richardt was stretched in a large leather chair smoking a cigar. Dr. Henck was huddled up at one end of the sofa. The door to the parlor stood open where Mrs. Henck and the children were lighting the Christmas tree. The dinner had been silent except for the happy chirping and prattle of the children.

'Why don't you say something, old man?' said Richardt. 'Are you sitting there thinking about your torn coat?'

'No,' answered Henck, 'rather about the fur coat.'

There was a silence and then he continued: 'I'm thinking of something else too – I'm thinking that this is the last

Christmas we shall ever celebrate together. I am a physician and I know that my days are numbered. I have thought that for some time and I'm sure of it now. So I want to thank you for all the kindnesses you have shown me – and my wife.'

'Oh, you're mistaken,' mumbled Richardt looking away.

'No,' answered Henck, 'I am not mistaken. And I want to thank you also for lending me your fur coat. It brought me the last happy moments I shall know in life.'

1923

THE EMPEROR'S VISION

Selma Lagerlöf

It happened at the time when Augustus was emperor in Rome and Herod was king in Jerusalem.

It was then that a very great and holy night sank down over the earth. It was the darkest night that anyone had ever seen. One could have believed that the whole earth had fallen into a cellar vault. It was impossible to distinguish water from land, and one could not find one's way on the most familiar road. And it couldn't be otherwise, for not a ray of light came from heaven. All the stars stayed at home in their own houses, and the fair moon held her face averted.

The silence and the stillness were as profound as the darkness. The rivers stood still in their courses, the wind did not stir, and even the aspen leaves had ceased to quiver. Had anyone walked along the seashore, he would have found that the waves no longer dashed upon the sands; and had one wandered in the desert, the sand would not have crunched under one's feet. Everything was as motionless as if turned to stone, so as not to disturb the holy night. The grass was afraid to grow, the dew could not fall, and the flowers dared not exhale their perfume.

On this night the wild beasts did not seek their prey, the serpents did not sting, and the dogs did not bark. And what was even more glorious, inanimate things would have been unwilling to disturb the night's sanctity by lending themselves to an evil deed. No false key could have picked a lock, and no knife could possibly have drawn a drop of blood.

In Rome, during this very night, a small company of people came from the emperor's palace at the Palatine and took the path across the Forum which led to the Capitol. During the day just ended, the senators had asked the emperor if he had any objections to their erecting a temple to him on Rome's sacred hill. But Augustus had not immediately given his consent. He did not know if it would be agreeable to the gods that he should own a temple next to theirs, and he had replied that first he wished to ascertain their will in the matter by offering a nocturnal sacrifice to his genius. It was he who, accompanied by a few trusted friends, was on his way to perform this sacrifice.

Augustus let them carry him in his litter, for he was old, and it was an effort for him to climb the long stairs leading to the Capitol. He himself held the cage with the doves for the sacrifice. No priests or soldiers or senators accompanied him, only his nearest friends. Torchbearers walked in front of him in order to light the way in the night darkness and behind him followed the slaves, who carried the tripod, the knives, the charcoal, the sacred fire, and all the other things needed for the sacrifice.

On the way the emperor chatted gaily with his faithful followers, and therefore none of them noticed the infinite silence and stillness of the night. Only when they had reached the highest point of the Capitol Hill and the vacant spot upon which they contemplated erecting the temple, did it dawn upon them that something unusual was taking place.

It could not be a night like all others, for up on the very edge of the cliff they saw the most remarkable being! At first they thought it was an old, distorted olive trunk; later they imagined that an ancient stone figure from the temple of Jupiter had wandered out on the cliff. Finally it was apparent to them that it could be only the old sibyl.

Anything so aged, so weather-beaten, and so giant-like in stature they had never seen. This old woman was

33

awe-inspiring! If the emperor had not been present, they would all have fled to their homes.

'It is she,' they whispered to one another, 'who has lived as many years as there are sand grains on her native shores. Why has she come out from her cave just tonight? What does she foretell for the emperor and the empire – she, who writes her prophecies on the leaves of the trees and knows that the wind will carry the words of the oracle to the person for whom they are intended?'

They were so terrified that they would have dropped on their knees with their foreheads pressed against the earth, had the sibyl stirred. But she sat as still as though she were lifeless. Crouching upon the outermost edge of the cliff, and shading her eyes with her hand, she peered out into the night. She sat there as if she had gone up on the hill that she might see more clearly something that was happening far away. She could see things on a night like this!

At that moment the emperor and all his retinue marked how profound the darkness was. None of them could see a hand's breadth in front of him. And what stillness! What silence! Not even the Tiber's hollow murmur could they hear. The air seemed to suffocate them, cold sweat broke out on their foreheads, and their hands were numb and powerless. They feared that some dreadful disaster was impending.

But no one dared to show that he was afraid, and everyone told the emperor that this was a good omen. All nature held its breath to greet a new god.

They counseled Augustus to hurry with the sacrifice, and said that the old sibyl had evidently come out of her cave to greet his genius.

But the truth was that the old sibyl was so absorbed in a vision that she did not even know Augustus had come up to the Capitol. She was transported in spirit to a far-distant land, where she imagined that she was wandering over a great plain. In the darkness she stubbed her foot continually against something, which she believed to be grass tufts. She stooped down and felt with her hand. No, it was not grass, but sheep. She was walking between great sleeping flocks of sheep.

Then she noticed the shepherds' fire. It burned in the middle of the field, and she groped her way to it. The shepherds lay asleep by the fire, and beside them were the long, spiked staves with which they defended their flocks from wild beasts. But the little animals with the glittering eyes and the bushy tails that stole up to the fire, were they not jackals? And yet the shepherds did not fling their staves at them, the dogs continued to sleep, the sheep did not flee, and the wild animals lay down to rest beside the human beings.

This the sibyl saw, but she knew nothing of what was being enacted on the hill at the back of her. She did not know that there they were raising an altar, lighting charcoal and strewing incense, and that the emperor took one of the doves from the cage to sacrifice it. But his hands were so benumbed that he could not hold the bird. With one stroke of the wing, it freed itself and disappeared in the night darkness.

When this happened, the courtiers glanced suspiciously at the old sibyl. They believed that it was she who caused the misfortune.

Could they know that all the while the sibyl thought herself standing beside the shepherds' fire, and that she listened to a faint sound that came trembling through the dead-still night? She heard it long before she marked that it did not come from the earth, but from the sky. At last she raised her head; then she saw light, shimmering forms glide forward in the darkness. They were little flocks of angels, who, singing joyously, and apparently searching, flew back and forth above the wide plain.

While the sibyl was listening to the angel song, the emperor was making preparations for a new sacrifice. He washed his hands, cleansed the altar, and took up the other dove. And although he exerted his full strength to hold it fast, the dove's slippery body slid from his hand, and the bird swung itself up into the impenetrable night.

The emperor was appalled! He fell upon his knees and prayed to his genius. He implored him for strength to avert the disasters that this night seemed to foreshadow.

Nor did the sibyl hear any of this either. She was listening with her whole soul to the angel song, which grew louder and louder. At last it became so powerful that it wakened the shepherds. They raised themselves on their elbows and saw shining hosts of silver-white angels move in the darkness in long, swaying lines, like migratory birds. Some held lutes and cymbals in their hands; others held zithers and harps, and their song rang out as merry as child-laughter, and as carefree as the lark's trill. When the shepherds heard this, they rose up to go to the mountain city, where they lived, to tell of the miracle.

They groped their way forward on a narrow, winding path, and the sibyl followed them. Suddenly it grew light up there on the mountain: a big, clear star kindled right over it, and the city on the mountain summit glittered like silver in the starlight. All the fluttering angel throngs hastened thither, shouting for joy, and the shepherds hurried so that they almost ran. When they reached the city, they found that the angels had assembled over a low stable near the city gate. It was a wretched structure, with a roof of straw and the naked cliff for a back wall. Over it hung the star, and hither flocked more and more angels. Some seated themselves on the straw roof or alighted upon the steep mountain wall at the back of the house; others, again, held themselves in the air on outspread wings, and hovered over it. High, high up, the air was illuminated by the shining wings.

The instant the star kindled over the mountain city, all nature awoke, and the men who stood upon Capitol Hill could not help seeing it. They felt fresh but caressing winds that traveled through space; delicious perfumes streamed up about them; trees swayed; the Tiber began to murmur; the stars twinkled; and suddenly the moon stood out in the sky and lit up the world. And out of the clouds the two doves came circling down and lighted upon the emperor's shoulders.

When this miracle happened, Augustus rose, proud and happy, but his friends and his slaves fell on their knees.

'Hail, Caesar!' they cried. 'Thy genius hath answered thee. Thou art the god who shall be worshipped on Capitol Hill!'

And this cry of homage, which the men in their transport gave as a tribute to the emperor, was so loud that the old sibyl heard it. It waked her from her visions. She rose from her place on the edge of the cliff, and came down among the people. It was as if a dark cloud had arisen from the abyss and rushed down the mountain height. She was terrifying in her extreme age! Coarse hair hung in matted tangles around her head, her joints were enlarged, and the dark skin, hard as the bark of a tree, covered her body with furrow upon furrow.

Potent and awe-inspiring, she advanced toward the emperor. With one hand she clutched his wrist, with the other she pointed toward the distant East.

'Look!' she commanded, and the emperor raised his eyes and saw. The vaulted heavens opened before his eyes, and his glance traveled to the distant Orient. He saw a lowly stable behind a steep rock wall, and in the open doorway a few shepherds kneeling. Within the stable he saw a young mother on her knees before a little child, who lay upon a bundle of straw on the floor.

And the sibyl's big, knotty fingers pointed toward the poor babe. 'Hail, Caesar!' cried the sibyl, in a burst of scornful laughter. 'There is the god who shall be worshipped on Capitol Hill!'

Then Augustus shrank back from her, as from a maniac. But upon the sibyl fell the mighty spirit of prophecy. Her dim eyes began to burn, her hands were stretched toward heaven, her voice was so changed that it seemed not to be her own, but rang out with such resonance and power that it could have been heard over the whole world. And she uttered words that she appeared to be reading among the stars.

'Upon Capitol Hill shall the Redeemer of the world be worshipped – *Christ* – but not frail mortals.'

When she had said this, she strode past the terror-stricken men, walked slowly down the mountain, and disappeared.

But on the following day, Augustus strictly forbade the people to raise any temple to him on Capitol Hill. In place of it he built a sanctuary to the new-born God-Child, and called it HEAVEN'S ALTAR – *Ara Coeli*.

1908

THE FIR TREE

Hans Christian Andersen

Far down in the forest, where the warm sun and the fresh air made a sweet resting place, grew a pretty little fir tree; and yet it was not happy, it wished so much to be tall like its companions — the pines and firs which grew around it. The sun shone, and the soft air fluttered its leaves, and the little peasant children passed by, prattling merrily, but the fir tree heeded them not.

Sometimes the children would bring a large basket of raspberries or strawberries, wreathed on a straw, seat themselves near the fir tree, and say, 'Is it not a pretty little tree?' which made it feel more unhappy than before. And yet all this while the tree grew a notch or joint taller every year; for by the number of joints in the stem of a fir tree we can discover its age. Still, as it grew, it complained, 'Oh! How I wish I were as tall as the other trees, then I would spread out my branches on every side, and my top would overlook the wide world. I should have the birds building their nests on my boughs, and when the wind blew, I should bow with stately dignity like my tall companions.'

The tree was so discontented, that it took no pleasure in the warm sunshine, the birds, or the rosy clouds that floated over it morning and evening. Sometimes, in winter, when the snow lay white and glittering on the ground, a hare would come springing along, and jump right over the little tree; and then how mortified it would feel! Two winters passed, and when the third arrived, the tree had grown so tall that the hare was obliged to run around it. Yet it remained unsatisfied, and would exclaim, 'Oh, if I could but keep on growing tall and old! There is nothing else worth caring for in the world!'

In the autumn, as usual, the woodcutters came and cut down several of the tallest trees, and the young fir tree, which was now grown to its full height, shuddered as the noble trees fell to the earth with a crash. After the branches were lopped off, the trunks looked so slender and bare, that they could scarcely be recognised. Then they were placed upon wagons, and drawn by horses out of the forest. 'Where were they going? What would become of them?' The young fir tree wished very much to know; so in the spring, when the swallows and the storks came, it asked, 'Do you know where those trees were taken? Did you meet them?'

The swallows knew nothing, but a stork, after a little reflection, nodded his head, and said, 'Yes, I think I do. I met several new ships when I flew from Egypt, and they had fine masts that smelled like fir. I think these must have been the trees; I assure you they were stately, very stately.'

'Oh, how I wish I were tall enough to go on the sea,' said the fir tree. 'What is the sea, and what does it look like?'

'It would take too much time to explain,' said the stork, flying quickly away.

'Rejoice in thy youth,' said the sunbeam, 'rejoice in thy fresh growth, and the young life that is in thee.'

And the wind kissed the tree, and the dew watered it with tears; but the fir tree regarded them not.

Christmastime drew near, and many young trees were cut down, some even smaller and younger than the fir tree who enjoyed neither rest nor peace with longing to leave its forest home. These young trees, which were chosen for their beauty, kept their branches, and were also laid on wagons and drawn by horses out of the forest.

'Where are they going?' asked the fir tree. 'They are not taller than I am: indeed, one is much less; and why are the branches not cut off? Where are they going?'

'We know, we know,' sang the sparrows, 'We have looked in at the windows of the houses in the town, and we know what is done with them. They are dressed up in the most splendid manner. We have seen them standing in the middle of a warm room, and adorned with all sorts of beautiful things: honey cakes, gilded apples, playthings, and many hundreds of wax tapers.'

'And then,' asked the fir tree, trembling through all its branches, 'and then what happens?'

'We did not see any more,' said the sparrows, 'but this was enough for us.'

'I wonder whether anything so brilliant will ever happen to me,' thought the fir tree. 'It would be much better than crossing the sea. I long for it almost with pain. Oh! When will Christmas be here? I am now as tall and well grown as those that were taken away last year. Oh! that I were now laid on the wagon, or standing in the warm room, with all that brightness and splendor around me! Something better and more beautiful is to come after, or the trees would not be so decked out. Yes, what follows will be grander and more splendid. What can it be? I am weary with longing. I scarcely know how I feel.'

'Rejoice with us,' said the air and the sunlight. 'Enjoy your own bright life in the fresh air.'

But the tree would not rejoice, though it grew taller every day; and, winter and summer, its dark-green foliage might be seen in the forest, while passersby would say, 'What a beautiful tree!'

A short time before Christmas, the discontented fir tree was the first to fall. As the axe cut through the stem, and divided the pith, the tree fell with a groan to the earth, conscious of pain and faintness, and forgetting all its anticipations of happiness, in sorrow at leaving its home in the forest. It knew that it should never again see its dear old companions, the trees, or the little bushes and multicolored flowers that had grown by its side; perhaps not even the birds. Neither was the journey at all pleasant. The tree first recovered itself while being unpacked in the courtyard of a house, with several other trees; and it heard a man say, 'We only want one, and this is the prettiest.'

Then came two servants in grand livery, and carried the fir tree into a large and beautiful apartment. On the walls hung pictures, and near the great stove stood great china vases, with lions on the lids. There were rocking chairs, silken sofas, large tables covered with pictures, books, and playthings, worth a great deal of money – at least, the children said so. Then the fir tree was placed in a large tub, full of sand; but green baize hung all around it, so that no one could see it was a tub, and it stood on a very handsome carpet. How the fir tree trembled! 'What was going to happen to him now?' Some young ladies came, and the servants helped them to adorn the tree. On one branch they hung little bags cut out of coloured paper, and each bag was filled with sweetmeats; from other branches hung gilded apples and walnuts, as if they had grown there; and above and all around were hundreds of red, blue, and white tapers, which were fastened on the branches. Dolls, exactly like real babies, were placed under the green leaves – the tree had never seen such things before – and at the very top was fastened a glittering star, made of tinsel. Oh, it was very beautiful!

'This evening,' they all exclaimed, 'how bright it will be!' 'Oh, that the evening were come,' thought the tree, 'and the tapers lighted! Then I shall know what else is going to happen. Will the trees of the forest come to see me? I wonder if the sparrows will peep in at the windows as they fly? Shall I grow faster here, and keep on all these ornaments summer and winter?' But guessing was of very little use; it made his bark ache, and this pain is as bad for a slender fir tree as a headache is for us. At last the tapers were lighted, and then what a glistening blaze of light the tree presented! It trembled so with joy in all its branches, that one of the candles fell among the green leaves and burned some of them. 'Help! help!' exclaimed the young ladies, but there was no danger, for they quickly extinguished the fire. After this, the tree tried not to tremble at all, though the fire frightened him; he was so anxious not to hurt any of the beautiful ornaments, even while their brilliance dazzled him. And now the folding doors were thrown open, and a troop of children rushed in as if they intended to upset the tree; they were followed more silently by their elders. For a moment the little ones stood silent with astonishment, and then they shouted for joy, till the room rang, and they danced merrily around the tree, while one present after another was taken from it.

'What are they doing? What will happen next?' thought the fir. At last the candles burned down to the branches and were put out. Then the children received permission to plunder the tree.

Oh, how they rushed upon it, till the branches cracked, and had it not been fastened with the glistening star to the ceiling, it would have been thrown down. The children then danced about with their pretty toys, and no one noticed the tree, except the children's maid who came and peeped among the branches to see if an apple or a fig had been forgotten.

'A story, a story,' cried the children, pulling a little fat man toward the tree.

'Now we shall be in the green shade,' said the man, as he seated himself under it, 'and the tree will have the pleasure of hearing also, but I shall only relate one story; what shall it be? "Ivede-Avede" or "Humpty Dumpty", who fell down stairs, but soon got up again, and at last married a princess.'

'"Ivede-Avede",' cried some. '"Humpty Dumpty",' cried others, and there was a fine shouting and crying out. But the fir tree remained quite still, and thought to himself, 'Shall I have anything to do with all this?' but he had already amused them as much as they wished. Then the old man told them the story of Humpty Dumpty, how he fell down stairs, and was raised up again, and married a princess. And the children clapped their hands and cried, 'Tell another, tell another,' for they wanted to hear the story of 'Ivede-Avede'; but they had only 'Humpty Dumpty.' After this the fir tree became quite silent and thoughtful; never had the birds in the forest told such tales as 'Humpty Dumpty', who fell down stairs, and yet married a princess.

'Ah! Yes, so it happens in the world,' thought the fir tree; he believed it all, because it was related by such a nice man. 'Ah! Well,' he thought, 'who knows? Perhaps I may fall down too, and marry a princess'; and he looked forward joyfully to the next evening, expecting to be again decked out with lights and playthings, gold and fruit. 'Tomorrow I will not tremble,' thought he; 'I will enjoy all my splendor, and I shall hear the story of Humpty Dumpty again, and perhaps Ivede-Avede.' And the tree remained quiet and thoughtful all night. In the morning the servants and the housemaid came in. 'Now,' thought the fir, 'all my splendor is going to begin again.' But they dragged him out of the room and upstairs to the garret, and threw him on the floor, in a dark corner, where no daylight shone, and there they left him. 'What does this mean?' thought the tree. 'What am I to do here? I can hear nothing in a place like this,' and he had time enough to think, for days and nights passed and no one came near him, and when at last somebody did come, it was only to put away large boxes in a corner. So the tree was completely hidden from sight as if it had never existed. 'It is winter now,' thought the tree, 'the ground is hard and covered with snow, so that people cannot plant me. I shall be sheltered here, I dare say, until spring comes. How thoughtful and kind everybody is to me! Still. I wish this place was not so dark, as well as lonely, with not even a little hare to look at. How pleasant it was out in the forest while the snow lay on the ground, when the hare would run by, yes, and jump over me too, although I did not like it then. Oh! It is terribly lonely here.'

'Squeak, squeak,' said a little mouse, creeping cautiously toward the tree; then came another; and they both sniffed at the fir tree and crept between the branches.

'Oh, it is very cold,' said the little mouse, 'or else we should be so comfortable here, shouldn't we, you old fir tree?'

'I am not old,' said the fir tree, 'there are many who are older than I am.'

'Where do you come from? And what do you know?' asked the mice, who were full of curiosity. 'Have you seen the most beautiful places in the world, and can you tell us all about them? And have you been in the storeroom, where cheeses lie on the shelf, and hams hang from the ceiling? One can run about on tallow candles there, and go in thin and come out fat.'

'I know nothing of that place,' said the fir tree, 'but I know the wood where the sun shines and the birds sing.' And then the tree told the little mice all about its youth. They had never heard such an account in their lives; and after they had listened to it attentively, they said, 'What a number of things you have seen! You must have been very happy.'

'Happy!' exclaimed the fir tree, and then as he reflected upon what he had been telling them, he said, 'Ah, yes! After all, those were happy days.' But when he went on and related all about Christmas Eve, and how he had been dressed up with cakes and lights, the mice said, 'How happy you must have been, you old fir tree.'

'I am not old at all,' replied the tree, 'I only came from the forest this winter; I am now checked in my growth.'

'What splendid stories you can relate,' said the little mice. And the next night four other mice came with them to hear what the tree had to tell. The more he talked the more he remembered, and then he thought to himself, 'Those were happy days, but they may come again. Humpty Dumpty fell down stairs, and yet he married the princess; perhaps I may marry a princess too.' And the fir tree thought of the pretty little birch tree that grew in the forest, which was to him a real beautiful princess.

'Who is Humpty Dumpty?' asked the little mice. And then the tree related the whole story; he could remember every single word, and the little mice were so delighted with it, that they were ready to jump to the top of the tree. The next night a great many more mice made their appearance, and on Sunday two rats came with them; but they said, it was not a pretty story at all, and the little mice were very sorry, for it made them also think less of it.

'Do you know only one story?' asked the rats.

'Only one,' replied the fir tree. 'I heard it on the happiest evening of my life; but I did not know I was so happy at the time.'

'We think it is a very miserable story,' said the rats. 'Don't you know any story about bacon, or tallow in the storeroom.'

'No,' replied the tree.

'Many thanks to you then,' replied the rats, and they marched off.

The little mice also kept away after this, and the tree sighed, and said, 'It was very pleasant when the merry little mice sat round me and listened while I talked. Now that is all passed too. However, I shall consider myself happy when someone comes to take me out of this place.' But would this ever happen?

Yes; one morning people came to clear out the garret, the boxes were packed away, and the tree was pulled out of the corner, and thrown roughly on the garret floor; then the servant dragged it out upon the staircase where the daylight shone. 'Now life is beginning again,' said the tree, rejoicing in the sunshine and fresh air. Then it was carried downstairs and taken into the courtyard so quickly that it forgot to think of itself, and could only look about, there was so much to be seen. The courtyard was close to a garden, where everything looked blooming. Fresh and fragrant roses hung over the little palings. The linden trees were in blossom; while the swallows flew here and there, crying, 'Twit, twit, twit, my mate is coming,' – but it was not the fir tree they meant. 'Now I shall live,' cried the tree, joyfully spreading out its branches; but alas! They were all withered and yellow, and it lay in a corner amongst weeds and nettles. The star of gold paper still stuck in the top of the tree and glittered in the sunshine. In the same courtyard two of the merry children were playing who had danced around the tree at Christmas, and had been so happy. The youngest saw the gilded star, and ran and pulled it off the tree. 'Look what is sticking to the ugly old fir tree,' said the child, treading on the branches till they crackled under his boots. And the tree saw all the fresh bright flowers in the garden, and then looked at itself, and wished it had remained in the dark corner of the garret. It thought of its fresh youth in the forest, of the merry Christmas evening, and of the little mice who had listened to the story of 'Humpty Dumpty'. 'Past! Past!' said the old tree; 'Oh, had I but enjoyed myself while I could have done so! But now it is too late.'

Then a lad came and chopped the tree into small pieces, till a large bundle lay in a heap on the ground. The pieces were placed in a fire under the copper, and they quickly blazed up brightly, while the tree sighed so deeply that each sigh was like a pistol shot. Then the children, who were at play, came and seated themselves in front of the fire, and looked at it and cried, 'Pop, pop.' But at each 'pop,' which was a deep sigh, the tree was thinking of a summer day in the forest; and of Christmas evening, and of 'Humpty Dumpty', the only story it had ever heard or knew how to relate, till at last it was consumed. The boys still played in the garden, and the youngest wore the golden star on his breast, with which the tree had been adorned during the happiest evening of its existence. Now all was past; the tree's life was past, and the story also – for all stories must come to an end at last.

1845

ANOTHER STAR

Ingvar Ambjørnsen

Lester called around ten o'clock. It was the night before Christmas Eve, and the streets in town were about to disappear under all the snow. A strong wind was blowing in from the fjord; it whipped the crystals into the smallest cracks, and formed a fairy-tale landscape out in the back-yard. I had been sitting in my chair by the window drinking red wine. I had probably reverted to my childhood, because something of a boy's enjoyment over a heavy snowfall blossomed in me. It was lovely to see the neighbour's gateway being slowly choked, becoming covered with all this whiteness. I sat there alone with my Christmas peace. The woodstove whistled and hissed by itself as the humidity in the birch logs was squeezed out through the flues.

I didn't want to answer the phone, but then I remembered that I had a frail mother in another part of the country.

As I said, it was Lester. He felt it was high time to share a Christmas star or two. And to my own surprise, I said yes. I got dressed at once and walked outside.

The town was almost deserted. Only from the bars could I hear noise and laughter. Lester lived in one of the old shacks down by the river. The streets were not ploughed there; I was walking in snow halfway up to my knees. When I arrived, I brushed the worst off before I went into the stairwell. He had left the door open a crack on the first floor. I could hear him rummaging around in the kitchen.

'You were sitting in your chair again, weren't you?' He was making himself a huge packed lunch. Slices of bread covered the whole table; he cut long yellow strips off the cheese.

'Yes,' I said.

'That chair will eat you one day. It's not just me who's worried.' I sat down on the log crate.

'This weather's quite a gift,' he continued. 'And the forest stands exactly where it stands, indeed.' I tried to get him to see that he had, indeed, gone mad.

'You make the tea,' he continued. 'Water's boiling.' He piled the slices of bread on top of one another, and made two huge parcels. Later we filled two two-litre thermoses with tea.

'I'm not dressed for any North Pole expedition,' I said.

'No,' he said. 'I know that.'

I shouldn't really have been surprised. I had known him for so long. Lester was a man of objects. The whole house was filled to the brim with furniture and lamps, brass candle-holders, paintings, carpets and ornaments. In the bedroom he had a closet the size of my own living room. But when he took me in there and showed me the two Italian pilot uniforms from the Second World War, I still became a little dumbfounded. I'd never seen an Italian pilot uniform before. It was sown as one piece, and from the crotch a zipper ran all the way up to the neck. The hood could be pulled down to the top of the eyes, and tied up. The uniforms were fully lined, both the legs and the sleeves, and they were stiff from green impregnation. When I'd managed to get into mine, I looked like the Michelin Man. The boots were original, too. They, too, were lined, and made of thick leather that Lester had greased with pork fat. They reached up to my knees, and when I folded the trouser legs over them and tied them, I was armed for the Pole journey I had talked about after all. A snowstorm here in Norway was no big deal. I helped Lester to put on his outfit. Then we took our backpacks and waddled back to the kitchen. It was hard to move. Your arms were pushed out from the body, and you automatically attained a broad gait.

Lester found the two red stars. They were tiny and lay sparkling in his sweaty hand. I recognised them from before, and felt they were safe. It was strong stuff, but with a somewhat speedy engine, which made it quite easy to keep control. We ate one each. Then we packed our backpacks and left.

Outside the weather had now gone totally insane. We had to lean into the wind. Now and then the gusts hit us with such force that we almost toppled over. I was still feeling warm and cosy behind my impregnated shield. When we were halfway to the town centre, Lester stopped and pulled off his backpack. He rummaged in it, and pulled out two pairs of goggles that belonged to the armour. We now looked completely and utterly like two Italian pilots from the Second World War. The plane was the only thing missing. I even had a pair of stripes on my sleeves, and a single distinction of some sort above the left breast pocket.

We caught the very last bus from the bus terminal. Every time we stopped to pick up new passengers, there were people who thought they were seeing things. The bus rose slowly up above the town, and its lights lay flickering beneath us in the sea of snow. In between the heavy trees we caught glimpses of lit-up windows in villas we couldn't see. We were the only ones who got off the bus at the last stop. The old bus turned and drove back. There were no houses up here, nothing but dark forest and white snow. When we took our first steps into this eerie witch's wood, I noticed the LSD seeping through me like a warm, electric quiver. Here there was no path. We cut in through the spruce trunks, and the white layer came up to our thighs. But it was colder up here in the hills. The snow was dry, and it was easy to wade through it. The contrast between the black forest and the white snow was overwhelming. We were moving inside a black-and-white film. The colours were dead, and that gave us a sense of great peace. We didn't talk; it wasn't necessary, besides it was impossible. The wind would sweep our words out into the nothingness before they reached the other person's ear. And I thought it was good this way. Good to walk in this wordless landscape of friendly spruce trees and piercing wind. The thought that only a couple of hours ago I was sitting in an armchair drinking wine, seemed absurd. This is where I belonged. I was an immense landscape, an ur-mensch; it breathed, I breathed in it, it breathed in me. As we got deeper into the forest, the snow was reaching up to our chests, we let ourselves fall forward, we sank down into the whiteness. I became a pupa; a fluid solution encapsulated in a shell; soon I would step forth as something new, something different. How utterly fed up I was with all those years I had behind me, years in the pupa phase, all the time which had been lost to meaningless word-wrangling.

After more than two hours we arrived at a cleared forest path. We brushed the snow off our pilot uniforms and continued into the nothingness. We had no idea where we were, just that we found ourselves at quite a distance from the social democratic control system, where two and two had a nasty habit of turning out to be four. We stopped somewhere to eat our sandwiches. They hit the spot ... I can't describe it, but I understood that it was the first real *bread* I had ever had in my mouth. I could clearly feel how the nourishment forced its way into my body as I chewed and swallowed.

We kept going. It was approaching five o'clock in the morning, and the twists of fate led us once more in the direction of civilization. The forest path we had followed turned into an avenue of villas; we suddenly found ourselves among the most expensive properties at the top of the ridge. One villa after the other became visible through the snowfall; they looked like huge UFOs, millionaire mansions from another planet. The yellow outdoor lights in entrances and entryways danced in front of our eyes, pulsated, grew, contracted. The top of the snowbanks were above our heads; it was like walking in a glittering tunnel.

Here! Lester thought. He didn't say it, I'm absolutely sure of that, and at that very moment I noticed how tired I was. We had a massive physical exertion behind us. Now our legs gave up on us. The acid was thumping around in my consciousness, I saw myself from outside, I saw that my own batteries were almost flat, saw the aura that contracted toward the body. I couldn't go on. I just wanted to sleep until next year.

Lester took off his backpack and took out his collapsible spade of light metal. It seemed so natural, I remember. Like all Norwegians, it came through our mothers' milk. Trouble in heavy snow? Dig yourself down. Dig yourself down in time. Lester attacked the snowbank, and I used my hands to help. He cut neat blocks out of the compact snow, and put them aside; they would form the outer wall. Later we dug ourselves straight in, before we continued at a sharp right angle.

It was another world. Another star. We lay next to each other on Lester's ground pad. The round concave roof above us made me think of the uterus I came from. It wasn't cold. We had lit a candle, and lay and watched the flame, and the shadows playing across the smooth walls. Because of the heat created by us and the candle, a thin layer of ice, a fine glazing, was forming over walls and ceiling. It was utterly impossible to grasp that we were actually lying in a cave in one of the town's most exclusive residential streets. Outside it was still dark, but now and then the odd car drove past. As they passed the covered-up cave entrance where the snow cover was at its thinnest, the front lights threw a warm glow into our room. There was something almost physical about that light, we could put our hands into it, fetch warmth from it.

Lester took out two more trips. We had one each. Then we fell asleep.

I had never experienced anything like it. Waking up from an LSD high. It's a state beyond anything else, because the memory of what you have ingested has totally gone. When you wake up in a snow cave under such conditions, you're instinctively one with the cave, it's a part of you, it has always been like that. For an infinite time, I, together with this strange figure next to me, the one who is another aspect of myself, have been here. Here I am in my own ur-form, the cave man, the embryo. The muffled sounds from outside, the lights sweeping across the arched ceiling every time something passes out there in the strangeness, that's everything I can't know anything about. I've no desire to be born one more time. I remember in details the sound and light shocks from the last time, the intense discomfort of physical existence in time and space.

Lester woke up, too. He said something. I don't know what, but it was green and pink. He lit the candle again, and I happened to glance at my watch. It was an amusing watch. When I moved my left arm back and forth, the green light from the luminescent hands trailed behind like thin threads. For some reason the watch showed four thirty. That didn't tell me much. I had no idea that I'd slept for almost twelve hours. In a residential area. In a snow cave in a snowbank. I was utterly and fully present in the here and now, bereft of morals, ideas, doubts and beliefs. I was here. In what was my own. The wall was smooth when I moved my hand over it. There was something sensual about this cold, this wetness. Now and then we could hear voices from people out on the road. They approached. Then they went away again. I didn't understand a word, but enjoyed lying like this in half-darkness listening to the melody of the language.

Time passed. Or time stood still. I don't know. We were in this vacuum. The candle burning. The sound of our own breaths. Our heartbeats. Then: heavy turns of a shovel. Someone was digging in the snowbank from the side facing the garden.

'Hello? Is someone there?'

Language comprehension returned. I was almost in tears, there was something painful about the fact that the blind melody of the words disappeared. The picture of myself as caveman, an embryo swaddled in white, disappeared.

'Hello?'

We didn't answer. We sat utterly motionless in the glow of the candle.

It was the voice of an adult man. He swore and dug.

The breakthrough came just at the angle between the narrow passageway and the cave itself. We saw a glimpse of the shiny spade; then the wall fell into the space, and the winter evening revealed itself to us. In the garden three people were buried in snow up to their knees. A man and a woman and a girl aged five or six. The man rested his arms on the spade and looked at us, while he kept shaking his head.

'I don't believe it,' he said. 'I refuse to believe what I'm seeing.'

'My God!' said the woman.

The child began to cry.

I could understand them. I won't claim otherwise. I could understand the crying child, the woman who called on the Lord, and the man who couldn't believe his own eyes. It's not every day you happen upon two Italian pilots from the Second World War in your own garden. Especially not sitting in a snow cave. On the other hand: Who's expecting everyday events on Christmas Eve itself?

'Take it easy,' Lester said. 'We're leaving.'

The man wanted to know who we were, and we explained it to him as best we could, even if I, personally, was not totally sure. Who is anyone, anyway?

'Did you sleep there last night?' the woman asked. 'Yes,' we did.

The child cried and cried.

'There, there,' the father said and rumpled his daughter's hair. And to us: 'It was Helene who found you. She saw the light flicker in the snow.'

'Thanks a lot,' Lester said. 'You remember the story about the three wisemen, who followed the light from the star?'

She nodded, sobbing.

'It's Christmas Eve,' the woman said. Then she checked herself, and threw herself into deep Christian waters. 'You shall not walk away from here on an empty stomach. The turkey's in the oven.'

The man looked embarrassed, but didn't protest.

'Nothing much happens up here,' she said. 'Everything stands still. It ...' She had been drinking much and fast, and the hand that cut the turkey was not quite steady. The set table was swimming in colours; I was clinging to a wineglass. Over in a corner of the living room the lit-up Christmas tree pulsated from electric lights and glass beads. The little lady had long ago waved goodbye to her fears, now she was drinking soda while she was studying us with curiosity. We had taken off our Italian pilot uniforms, but we were still from another planet.

'Nothing much's happening anywhere,' Lester said. 'It's snowing and blowing. Now and then Christmas comes.'

'Well, cheers!' the man said.

We clinked glasses. It was good wine from their own cellar.

'I must say!' said the man. 'When I tell them this at work. That you ...' He laughed happily.

The turkey swelled in my mouth. For some reason the burning candles on the table made me think about Christ.

'Imagine!' she said. 'That you slept there all night.'

'Yes,' I said. 'And you slept in here. It's a strange world.'

'Afterwards we must dance around the Christmas tree,' the child said. 'And sing all the songs.'

'You can bet on it!' Lester said.

We danced around the tree. We sang all the songs. The woman got drunker and drunker, but she had good manners, and pulled herself together.

Then there were the presents. The sound of the crackling paper. The colours. Red, green and blue crackling in my brain. The man of the house had, inexplicably, managed to smuggle two bottles of vintage wine under the tree. This touched me, I burst into tears, while Lester was already building a medieval castle with the little girl's Lego set. I walked into the hallway and cut the distinctions out of my pilot uniform. I gave them to the man, at the same time as I explained to him that he now had a new hobby. My knife I gave to the little girl, who was now Lester's best friend and master builder. I wanted to give my silver ring to the woman, but she had withdrawn. I saw her in my mind's eye, lying across a double bed somewhere far inside the large villa.

The man and I sat and talked past each other for a few hours, while we laboriously worked our way through his wine cellar. I became more and more sober for each glass; it was the LSD pulling out of me. Lester was still high; far into his own world of builders. He was working on the eastern tower now, while he constantly reeled off intricate fairy tales linked with the castle. The little girl sat there with big round eyes and open mouth.

Finally I'd had enough. The man had a good heart, but a social intelligence which allowed him only to circle around French vineyards, plus the importation of luxury cars. Besides, as he got more and more wasted, he entered into a self-reproaching phase, in which he aimed at making me understand that he regretted having arranged his life the way he had. From now on, to hell with material comforts. To hell with status, stress and false friendships. As a young man he'd been very good at drawing. Now he wanted to start drawing again. He wanted to shove the whole job where it belonged, and then he would seriously start to draw. Quite simply, he would become like Lester and me. He probably took it for granted that we dabbled in the arts, as our hair was so messy, and besides, we were walking around in Italian pilot uniforms from the Second World War.

I said goodbye. I can't stand millionaires who hate themselves when they get drunk. I just had to give up on Lester; he'd become a little boy again, and would probably stay like that for the rest of the night.

Outside there was utter silence. Starry sky, and cracklingly cold. I looked forward to the long walk down to the town centre. When I passed the snow cave, I saw that the candle was lit again.

She was crouching, dressed in Lester's pilot uniform, a bottle of sherry in her hand. Her lips were constantly moving. It was impossible to hear what she said, but later I've enjoyed imagining that she sat there and told herself what her real name was.

2003

ROUND THE YULE LOG

Peter Christen Asbjørnsen

The wind was whistling through the old lime and maple trees opposite my windows, the snow was sweeping down the street, and the sky was black as a December sky can possibly be here in Christiania. I was in just as black a mood. It was Christmas Eve – the first I was to spend away from the cosy fireside of my home. I had lately received my officer's commission, and had hoped that I should have gladdened my aged parents with my presence during the holidays, and had also hoped that I should be able to show myself in all my glory and splendor to the ladies of our parish. But a fever had brought me to the hospital, which I had left only a week before, and now I found myself in the much-extolled state of convalescence. I had written home for a horse and sledge and my father's fur coat, but my letter could scarcely reach our valley before the day after Christmas, and the horse could not be in town before New Year's Eve.

My comrades had all left town, and I knew no family with whom I could make myself at home during the holidays. The two old maids I lodged with were certainly very kind and friendly people, and they had taken great care of me in the commencement of my illness, but the peculiar ways and habits of these ladies were too much of the old school to prove attractive to the fancies of youth. Their thoughts dwelled mostly on the past; and when they, as often might occur, related to me some stories of the town, its people and its customs, these stories reminded me, not only by their contents, but also by the simple, unaffected way in which they were rendered, of a past age.

The antiquated appearance of these ladies was also in the strictest harmony with the house in which they lived. It was one of those old houses on Custom House Street, with deep windows, long dark passages and staircases, gloomy rooms and garrets, where one could not help thinking of ghosts and brownies; in short, just such a house, and perhaps it was the very one, that Mauritz Hansen has described in his story, 'The Old Dame with the Hood.' Their circle of acquaintances was very limited;

besides a married sister and her children, no other visitors came there but a couple of tiresome old ladies. The only relief to this kind of life was a pretty niece and some merry little cousins of hers, who always made me tell them fairy tales and stories.

I tried to divert myself in my loneliness and melancholy mood by looking out at all the people who passed up and down the street in the snow and wind, with blue noses and half-shut eyes. It amused me to see the bustle and the life in the apothecary's shop across the street. The door was scarcely shut for a moment. Servants and peasants streamed in and out, and commenced to study the labels and directions when they came out in the street. Some appeared to be able to make them out, but sometimes a lengthy study and a dubious shake of the head showed that the solution was too difficult. It was growing dusk. I could not distinguish the countenances any longer, but gazed across at the old building. The apothecary's house, 'The Swan,' as it is still called, stood there, with its dark, reddish-brown walls, its pointed gables and towers, with weathercocks and latticed windows, as a monument of the architecture of the time of King Christian the Fourth. The Swan looked then, as now, a most respectable and sedate bird, with its gold ring around its neck, its spur-boots, and its wings stretched out as if to fly. I was about to plunge myself into reflection on imprisoned birds when I was disturbed by noise and laughter proceeding from some children in the adjoining room, and by a gentle, old-maidish knock at my door.

On my requesting the visitor to come in, the elder of my landladies, Miss Mette, entered the room with a courtesy in the good old style; she inquired after my health, and invited me, without further ceremony, to come and make myself at home with them for the evening. 'It isn't good for you, dear Lieutenant, to sit thus alone here in the dark,' she added. 'Will you not come in to us now at once? Old Mother Skau and my brother's little girls have come; they will perhaps amuse you a little. You are so fond of the dear children.'

I accepted the friendly invitation. As I entered the room, the fire from the large square stove, where the logs were burning lustily, threw a red, flickering light through the wide-open door over the room, which was very deep, and furnished in the old style, with high-back, Russia leather chairs, and one of those settees which were intended for farthingales and straight up-and-down positions. The walls were adorned with oil paintings, portraits of stiff ladies with powdered coiffures, of bewigged Oldenborgians, and other redoubtable persons in mail and armour or red coats.

'You must really excuse us, Lieutenant, for not having lighted the candles yet,' said Miss Cicely, the younger sister, who was generally called 'Cilly,' and who came toward me and dropped a courtesy, exactly like her sister's; 'but the children do so like to tumble about here before the fire in the dusk of the evening, and Madam Skau does also enjoy a quiet little chat in the chimney corner.'

'Oh, chat me here and chat me there! There is nothing you like yourself better than a little bit of gossip in the dusk of the evening, Cilly, and then we are to get the blame of it,' answered the old asthmatic lady whom they called Mother Skau.

'Eh! Good evening, sir,' she said to me, as she drew herself up to make the best of her own inflated, bulky appearance. 'Come and sit down here and tell me how it fares with you; but, by my troth, you are nothing but skin and bones!'

I had to tell her all about my illness, and in return I had to endure a very long and circumstantial account of her rheumatism and her asthmatic ailments, which, fortunately, was interrupted by the noisy arrival of the children from the kitchen, where they had paid a visit to old Stine, a fixture in the house.

'Oh, Auntie, do you know what Stine says?' cried a little brown-eyed beauty. 'She says I shall go with her into the hayloft tonight and give the brownie his Christmas porridge. But I won't go; I am afraid of the brownies!'

'Never mind, my dear, Stine says it only to get rid of you; she dare not go into the hayloft herself – the foolish old thing – in the dark, for she knows well enough she was frightened once by the brownies herself,' said Miss Mette. 'But are you not going to say good evening to the Lieutenant, children?'

'Oh, is that you, Lieutenant?_I did not know you. How pale you are! It is such a long time since I saw you!' shouted the children all at once, as they flocked around me.

'Now you must tell us something awfully jolly! It is such a long time since you told us anything. Oh, tell us about Buttercup, dear Mr. Lieutenant, do tell us about Buttercup and Goldentooth!'

I had to tell them about Buttercup and the dog Goldentooth, but they would not let me off until I gave them a couple of stories into the bargain about the brownies at Vager and at Bure, who stole hay from each other, and who met at last with a load of hay on their backs, and how they fought till they vanished in a cloud of hay-dust. I had also to tell them the story of the brownie at Hesselberg, who teased the house dog till the farmer came out and threw him over the barn bridge. The children clapped their hands in great joy and laughed heartily.

'It served him right, the naughty brownie!' they shouted, and asked for another story.

'Well,' said I, 'I will tell you the story of Peter Gynt and the trolls.

In the olden days there lived in Kvam a hunter whose name was Peter Gynt, and who was always roaming about in the mountains after bears and elks, for in those days there were more forests on the mountains than there are now, and consequently plenty of wild beasts.

One day, shortly before Christmas, Peter set out on an expedition. He had heard of a farm on Doorefell which was invaded by such a number of trolls every Christmas Eve that the people on the farm had to move out, and get shelter at some of their neighbours. He was anxious to go there, for he had a great fancy to come across the trolls, and see if he could not overcome them. He dressed himself in some old ragged clothes, and took a tame white bear which he had with him, as well as an awl, some pitch and twine. When he came to the farm he went in and asked for lodgings.

'God help us!' said the farmer. 'We can't give you any lodgings. We have to clear out of the house ourselves soon and look for lodgings, for every Christmas Eve we have the trolls here.'

But Peter thought he should be able to clear the trolls out – he had done such a thing before; and then he got leave to stay, and a pig's skin into the bargain. The bear lay down behind the fireplace, and Peter took out his awl and pitch and twine, and began making a big, big shoe, which it took the whole pig's skin to make. He put a strong rope in for lacings, that he might pull the shoe tightly together, and, finally, he armed himself with a couple of handspikes.

Shortly he heard the trolls coming. They had a fiddler with them, and some began dancing, while others fell to eating the Christmas fare on the table – some fried bacon, and some fried frogs and toads, and other nasty things which they had brought with them. During this some of the trolls found the shoe Peter had made. They thought it must belong to a very big foot. They all wanted to try it on at once, so they put a foot each into it; but Peter made haste and tightened the rope, took one of the hand-spikes and fastened the rope around it, and got them at last securely tied up in the shoe.

Just then the bear put his nose out from behind the fireplace, where he was lying, and smelled they were frying something.

'Will you have a sausage, pussycat?' said one of the trolls, and threw a hot frog right into the bear's jaws.

'Scratch them, pussycat!' said Peter.

The bear got so angry that he rushed at the trolls and scratched them all over, while Peter took the other hand-spike and hammered away at them as if he wanted to beat their brains out. The trolls had to clear out at last, but Peter stayed and enjoyed himself with all the Christmas fare the whole week. After that the trolls were not heard of there for many years.

Some years afterward, about Christmas time, Peter was out in the forest cutting wood for the holidays, when a troll came up to him and shouted:

'Have you got that big pussy of yours, yet?'

'Oh, yes! She is at home behind the fireplace,' said he, 'and she has got seven kittens, all bigger and larger than herself.'

'We'll never come to you anymore, then,' said the troll, and they never did.

The children were all delighted with this story.

'Tell us another, dear Lieutenant,' they all shouted in chorus.

'No, no, children! You bother the Lieutenant too much,' said Miss Cicely. 'Aunt Mette will tell you a story now.'

'Yes, do, Auntie, do!' was the general cry.

'I don't know exactly what I shall tell you,' said Aunt Mette, 'but since we have commenced telling about the brownies, I think I will tell you something about them, too. You remember, of course, old Kari Gausdal, who came here and baked bread, and who always had so many tales to tell you.'

'Oh, yes, yes!' shouted the children.

'Well, old Kari told me that she was in service at the orphan asylum some years ago, and at that time it was still more dreary and lonely in that part of the town than it is now. That asylum is a dark and dismal place, I can tell you. Well, when Kari came there she was cook, and a very smart and clever girl she was. She had, one day, to get up very early in the morning to brew, when the other servants said to her, "You had better mind you don't get up too early, and you mustn't put any fire under the copper before two o'clock."

'"Why?" she asked.

'"Don't you know there is a brownie here? And you ought to know that those people don't like to be disturbed so early," they said, "and before two o'clock you mustn't light the fire by any means."

'"Is that all?" said Kari. She was anything but chicken hearted. 'I have nothing to do with that brownie of yours, but if he comes in my way, why, by my faith, I will send him head over heels through the door.'

'The others warned her, but she did not care a bit, and next morning, just as the clock struck one, she got up and lighted the fire under the copper in the brew house; but the fire went out in a moment. Somebody appeared to be throwing the logs about on the hearth, but she could not see who it was. She gathered the logs together, one at a time, but it was of no use, and the chimney would not draw, either. She got tired of this at last, took a burning log and ran around the room with it, swinging it high and low while she shouted, "Be gone, be gone whence you came! If you think you can frighten me you are mistaken." "Curse you!" somebody hissed in one of the darkest corners. "I have had seven souls in this house; I thought I should have got eight in all!"'

'"But from that time nobody saw or heard the brownie in the asylum," said Kari Gausdal.'

'I am getting so frightened!' said one of the children. 'No, you must tell us some more stories, Lieutenant; I never feel afraid when you tell us anything, because you tell us such jolly tales.' Another proposed that I should tell them about the brownie who danced the Halling dance with the lassie. That was a tale I didn't care much about, as there was some singing in it. But they would on no account let me off, and I was going to clear my throat and prepare my exceedingly inharmonious voice to sing the Halling dance, which belongs to the story, when the pretty niece, whom I have already referred to, entered the room, to the great joy of the children and to my rescue.

'Well, my dear children, I will tell you the story, if you can get cousin Lizzie to sing the Halling for you,' said I, as she sat down, 'and then you'll dance to it yourselves, won't you?'

Cousin Lizzie was besieged by the children, and had to promise to do the singing, so I commenced my story.

There was, once upon a time − I almost think it was in Hallingdal − a lassie who was sent up into the hayloft with the cream porridge for the brownie − I cannot recollect if it was on a Thursday or on a Christmas Eve, but I think it was a Christmas Eve. Well, she thought it was a great pity to give the brownie such a dainty dish, so she ate the porridge herself, and the melted butter in the bargain, and went up into the hayloft with the plain oatmeal porridge and sour milk, in a pig's trough instead. 'There, that's good enough for you, Master Brownie,' she said. But no sooner had she spoken the words than the brownie stood right before her, seized her around the waist and danced about with her, which he kept up till she lay gasping for breath, and when the people came up into the hayloft in the morning, she was more dead than alive. But as long as they danced, the brownie sang, (and here Cousin Lizzie undertook his part, and sang to the tune of the Halling):

'And you have eaten the porridge for the brownie, And you shall dance with the little brownie!

'And have you eaten the porridge for the brownie? Then you shall dance with the little brownie!'

I assisted in keeping time by stamping on the floor with my feet, while the children romped about the room in uproarious joy.

'I think you are turning the house upside down, children!' said old Mother Skau. 'If you'll be quiet, I'll give you a story.'

The children were soon quiet, and Mother Skau commenced as follows: 'You hear a great deal about brownies and fairies and such like beings, but I don't believe there is much in it. I have neither seen one nor the other. Of course I have not been so very much about in my lifetime, but I believe it is all nonsense. But old Stine out in the kitchen there, she says she has seen the brownie. About the time when I was confirmed she was in service with my parents. She came to us from a captain's, who had given up the sea. It was a very quiet place. The captain only took a walk as far as the quay every day. They always went to bed early. People said there was a brownie in the house. Well, it so happened that Stine and the cook were sitting in their room one evening, mending and darning their things. It was near bedtime, for the watchman had already sung out "Ten o'clock!" but somehow the darning and the sewing went on very slowly indeed; every moment "Jack Nap" came and played his tricks upon them. At one moment Stine was nodding and nodding, and then came the cook's turn – they could not keep their eyes open; they had been up early that morning to wash clothes. But just as they were sitting thus, they heard a terrible crash downstairs in the kitchen, and Stine shouted, "Lor' bless and preserve us! It must be the brownie." She was so frightened she dared scarcely move a foot, but at last the cook plucked up courage and went down into the kitchen, closely followed by Stine. When they opened the kitchen door they found all the crockery on the floor, but none of it broken, while the brownie was standing on the big kitchen table with his red cap on, and hurling one dish after the other on to the floor, and laughing in great glee. The cook had heard that the brownies could sometimes be tricked into moving into another house when anybody would tell them of a very quiet place, and as she long had been wishing for an opportunity to play a trick upon this brownie, she took courage and spoke to him – her voice was a little shaky at the time – that he ought to remove to the tinman's over the way, where it was so very quiet and pleasant, because they always went to bed at nine o'clock every evening; which was true enough, as the cook told Stine later, but then the master and all his apprentices and journeymen were up every morning at three o'clock and hammered away and made a terrible noise all day. Since that day they have not seen the brownie anymore at the captain's. He seemed to feel quite at home at the tinman's, although they were hammering and tapping away there all day; but people said that the goodwife put a dish of porridge up in the garret for him every Thursday evening, and it's no wonder that they got on well and became rich when they had a brownie in the house. Stine believed he brought things to them. Whether it was the brownie or not who really helped them, I cannot say,' said Mother Skau, in conclusion, and got a fit of coughing and choking after the exertion of telling this, for her, unusually long story.

When she had taken a pinch of snuff she felt better, and became quite cheerful again, and began: 'My mother, who, by the way, was a truthful woman, told a story that happened here in the town one Christmas Eve. I know it is true, for an untrue word never passed her lips.'

'Let us hear it, Madame Skau,' said I.

'Yes, tell, tell, Mother Skau!' cried the children.

She coughed a little, took another pinch of snuff, and proceeded: 'When my mother still was in her teens, she sometimes used to visit a widow whom she knew, and whose name was – dear me, what was her name? – Madame – yes, Madame Evensen, of course. She was a woman who had seen the best part of her life, but whether she lived up on Mill Street or down in the corner by the Little Church Hill, I cannot say for certain. Well, one Christmas Eve, just like tonight, she thought she would go to the morning service on Christmas Day, for she was a great churchgoer, and so she left out some coffee with the girl before she went to bed, that she might get a cup next morning – she was sure a cup of warm coffee would do her a great deal of good at that early hour. When she woke, the moon was shining into the room; but when she got up to look at the clock she found it had stopped and that the fingers pointed to half-past eleven. She had no idea what time it could be, so she went to the window and looked across to the church. The light was streaming out through all the windows. She must have overslept! She called the girl and told her to get the coffee ready, while she dressed herself. So she took her hymnbook and started for church. The street was very quiet; she did not meet a single person on her way to church. When she went inside, she sat down in her customary seat in one of the pews, but when she looked around her she thought that the people were so pale and so strange

– exactly as if they were all dead. She did not know any of them, but there were several of them she seemed to recollect having seen before; but when and where she had seen them she could not call to mind. When the minister came into the pulpit, she saw that he was not one of the ministers in the town, but a tall, pale man, whose face, however, she thought she could recollect. He preached very nicely indeed, and there was not the usual noisy coughing and hawking which you always hear at the morning services on a Christmas Day; it was so quiet, you could have heard a needle drop on the floor – in fact, it was so quiet she began to feel quite uneasy and uncomfortable. When the singing commenced again, a female who sat next to her leaned toward her and whispered in her ear, "Throw the cloak loosely around you and go, because if you wait here till the service is over they will make short work of you. It is the dead who are keeping service."'

'Oh, Mother Skau, I feel so frightened, I feel so frightened!' whimpered one of the children, and climbed up on a chair.

'Hush, hush, child!' said Mother Skau. 'She got away from them safe enough; only listen! When the widow heard the voice of the person next to her, she turned round to look at her – but what a start she got! She recognised her; it was her neighbour who died many years ago; and when she looked around the church, she remembered well that she had seen both the minister and several of the congregation before, and that they had died long ago. This sent quite a cold shiver through her, she became that frightened. She threw the cloak loosely round her, as the female next to her had said, and went out of the pew; but she thought they all turned around and stretched out their hands after her. Her legs shook under her, till she thought she would sink down on the church floor. When she came out on the steps, she felt that they had got hold of her cloak; she let it go and left it in their clutches, while she hurried home as quickly as she could. When she came to the door the clock struck one, and by the time she got inside she was nearly half-dead – she was that frightened. In the morning when the people went to church, they found the cloak lying on the steps, but it was torn into a thousand pieces. My mother had often seen the cloak before, and I think she saw one of the pieces, also; but that doesn't matter – it was a short, pink, woolen cloak, with fur lining and borders, such as was still in use in my childhood. They are very rarely seen nowadays, but there are some old ladies in the town and down at the "Home" whom I see with such cloaks in church at Christmastime.'

The children, who had expressed considerable fear and uneasiness during the latter part of the story, declared they would not hear any more such terrible stories. They had crept up onto the sofa and on the chairs, but still they thought they felt somebody plucking at them from underneath the table. Suddenly the lights were brought in, and we discovered then, to our great amusement, that the children had put their legs onto the table. The lights, the Christmas cake, the jellies, the tarts and the wine soon chased away the horrible ghost story and all fear from their minds, revived everybody's spirits and brought the conversation on to their neighbours and the topics of the day. Finally, our thoughts took a flight toward something more substantial, on the appearance of the Christmas porridge and the roast ribs of pork. We broke up early, and parted with the best wishes for a merry Christmas. I passed, however, a very uneasy night. I do not know whether it was the stories, the substantial supper, my weak condition or all these combined, which was the cause of it; I tossed myself hither and thither in my bed, and got mixed up with brownies, fairies and ghosts the whole night. Finally, I sailed through the air toward the church, while some merry sledge-bells were ringing in my ears. The church was lighted up, and when I came inside I saw it was our own church up in the valley. There was nobody there but peasants in their red caps, soldiers in full uniform, country lasses with their white headdresses and red cheeks. The minister was in the pulpit; it was my grandfather, who died when I was a little boy. But just as he was in the middle of the sermon, he made a somersault – he was known as one of the smartest men in the parish – right into the middle of the church; the surplice flew one way and the collar another. 'There lies the parson, and here am I,' he said, with one of his well-known airs, 'and now let us have a spring dance!' In an instant the whole of the congregation was in the midst of a wild dance. A big tall peasant came toward me and took me by the shoulder and said, 'You'll have to join us, my lad!'

At this moment I awoke, and felt someone pulling at my shoulder. I could scarcely believe my eyes when I saw the same peasant whom I had seen in my dream leaning over me. There he was, with the red cap down over his ears, a big fur coat over his arm and a pair of big eyes looking fixedly at me.

'You must be dreaming,' he said, 'the perspiration is standing in big drops on your forehead, and you were sleeping as heavily as a bear in his lair! God's peace and a merry Christmas to you, I say! And greetings to you from your father and all yours up in the valley. Here's a letter from your father, and the horse is waiting for you out in the yard.'

'But good heavens! Is that you, Thor?' I shouted in great joy. It was indeed my father's man, a splendid specimen of a Norwegian peasant. 'How in the world have you come here already?'

'Ah! that I can soon tell you,' answered Thor. 'I came with your favorite, the bay mare. I had to take your father down to Næs, and then he says to me, "Thor," says he, "it isn't very far to town from here. Just take the bay mare and run down and see how the Lieutenant is, and if he is well and can come back with you, you must bring him back along with you," says he.'

When we left the town it was daylight. The roads were in splendid condition. The bay mare stretched out her old smart legs, and we arrived at length in sight of the dear old house. Thor jumped off the sledge to undo the gate, and as we merrily drove up to the door we were met by the boisterous welcome of old Rover, who, in his frantic joy at hearing my voice, almost broke his chains in trying to rush at me.

Such a Christmas as I spent that year I cannot recollect before or since.

1895

THE FOREST WITCH

Johan Krohn

It was in the earliest springtime. In the shade the air was still quite cold; but where the clear and strong sunshine streamed down, one could see that spring had come, for there the blossoms were beginning to stretch upward on their tiny stalks.

A couple of children were walking through the forest: a ten-year-old girl named Nina and her little brother Johannes.

They were seeking flowers. Nina had to find them because the flowers were too tiny and much too hidden for so small a child as Johannes to discover them for himself, but she always let him have the pleasure of picking them.

It was such a joyous spring walk that Nina did not notice how far they were straying away from their grandmother's hut, at the back of the hill. This little hut had been their home only for a short time. When their dear father and mother died, their grandmother had kindly taken them to live with her and this was their first walk in the forest.

At last Nina thought they ought to go back, but just as she turned around with Johannes by the hand, who should stand before them but a hideous old creature, more glaring and frightful than you can imagine!

'What are you doing here, you wretched children?' she shrieked. 'Are you plucking flowers in my forest? Then shall I pluck you, you may believe!'

'Oh, pardon us,' cried Nina, 'we did not know that we must not pick flowers here. We are strangers in this forest. Pray, pray pardon us.'

'*Snikkesnak!*' answered the terrific old witch, for such the creature was. 'Don't talk to me! I never pay any attention to what children say; nor to old folks' talk either, for that matter. Indeed I don't! *Snikkesnak! Snikkesnak!* But it is not you that I want, silly girl. It is the boy there who has offended me. The little rascal! It is he who picked the flowers. Now I shall take him!'

'Oh! Take me, take me instead,' cried Nina in terror, flinging her arms around her brother. 'It is my fault! I showed him the flowers, and let him pick them. You've no right to take him! Oh! Do take me; he is too little.'

'*Snikkesnak!*' answered the witch. 'What a lot of talk! But you are right; the boy is small to come into my service, so I suppose I shall have to take you. Now listen well to what I say. Spring and summer are coming and I shall have no work for you then; so I shall not trouble myself about you for the present. But when autumn has come and gone, and all the leaves and flowers have disappeared, then are we very busy in the underground world. Then you may believe that I shall teach you how to work! And I live deep down, very, very deep! Now you may go; but I will make a bargain with you. When the last flower is faded – listen! – when the last flower is faded, meet me here on this spot – or ... or ...'

The old witch stopped to think what she could best threaten Nina with. Her wicked eyes glared around for an instant till she noticed that Nina stood, with her arms about her little brother, ready to ward off any evil that might come upon him.

'Or I shall come and catch this little rascal, and twist his arms and legs all out of joint!' screamed the witch, shaking her knotty stick at little Johannes.

Then, after a dark glance at Nina, she shuffled off through the forest, with the crows shrieking after her, and the leaves and flowers trembling on every side.

As soon as the witch was out of sight, Nina hastened home with Johannes. Like a kind sister she suited her frightened pace to his, so that he should not stumble and fall.

The poor little boy had been so terrified at the witch that he had not in the least understood the cruel threats she had used against him, or the dreadful fate that was in store for Nina.

Nina was rejoiced that this was so; for then he could not tell their grandmother what the witch had said, and she herself would not disclose the dreadful doom hanging over her. She was determined that the poor grandmother should not be made anxious and sorrowful as long as it could be helped.

Shortly after this, the spring burst forth in all its power and beauty, and the blossoms shot up everywhere – in the woods, the fields, the meadows, and the gardens. Nina welcomed them as her dearest friends. They would protect her against the forest witch. So long as she had a single one of these, she would not have to go down into the dark earth to serve the hideous creature.

Nina had always loved flowers, but never had she thought so much about them as now. Yet alas! Spring soon turned into summer, and summer went faster than ever before, it seemed to poor Nina. The tears streamed down her cheeks as she saw the blue cornflowers fall before the reaper's scythe, when the grain was cut in harvest time.

But Nina could still hope, even then; for the roses continued to bloom on Grandmother's old rose bush outside the door of the hut. Nina kissed them and begged them to last as long as ever they could! And so they did – the dear, friendly roses!

When the last little rose had at length withered, autumn had almost passed and the many-coloured leaves were dropping from the trees by the thousands. Yet Nina discovered to her joy and comfort that there were flowers still. Along the roadside stood the simple, hardy wild aster, which blossomed on and on, although the autumn winds and rains destroyed everything else.

Winter began, but so mildly that it seemed as if it were still autumn. When the asters finally disappeared, other help came to Nina; for the hazel bush was completely hoaxed by the mild weather and thought it was spring; so it began to unfold its yellow catkins, standing beautiful and bright, as one saw it between the bare trees over the hedges.

So, even when the winter was far advanced, Nina was still saved from going to the witch; but this could not long continue. Cold weather must soon come, because Grandmother had said that Christmas was near.

And suddenly winter did come in earnest, with its icy frosts and drifting snows. For five days it was impossible to get out of the hut, because the wind kept whirling the snow into high drifts all about it. But when the sixth day came the wind abated and the snow lay peacefully on the ground.

Now Nina dared no longer to stay in the house, for surely all the flowers were dead and buried under the cold snow after this bitter storm. She must go and keep her compact with the witch. So gathering together all her courage, she stole out of the house without being seen by anyone.

Outside, she stood still for an instant, took a last look at the hut, which now seemed so cosy and dear, whispered, 'Farewell', and started on her way to the forest.

But she had gathered too little courage, after all; for it melted away immediately when she discovered the witch a few steps from the door, standing in the little roadside garden, waiting for her.

'You've been rather slow about keeping to your bargain!' exclaimed the witch angrily. 'I was just coming after you.'

'Oh! Do not make me go with you!' cried Nina.

In her agony she fell down upon the snow at the witch's great feet, and besought her wildly: 'Let me be free! Oh, do let me be free!'

'Snikkesnak!' snapped the witch. 'Up with you! No nonsense!'

'Is there not a single flower to save me?' wailed Nina. She half rose, and, fairly beside herself with fright and despair, began to scrape the snow away from the garden bed at the side of the path, trying to find a flower.

'Oh, yes, look if you like! *Snikkesnak! Snikkesnak!*' laughed the witch, her face glowing with exultation at Nina's trouble.

But an instant after, her countenance became filled with fury, for where Nina had cleared the snow away, there appeared a plant with fresh dark green leaves and white flower buds!

Nina clasped her hands together in great joy and thankfulness; then, breaking off a bud, she lifted it up high toward the witch and rushed away into the hut. The witch, in her disappointment and vexation, sprang about so wildly in the snow that it rose in a cloud all about her, and Nina never saw her again.

Safe at home in the little hut, Nina now told all her adventure; and the grandmother took the little girl's sweet, frightened face between her two old hands, and kissed her forehead many times.

Faithfully every day Nina went to pay a loving visit to the little 'Christmas Rose' in the garden, for that was the flower that had saved her; and the whole winter long, it could be found fresh and beautiful, here and there under the snow.

Though no other blossoms dare come forth to face the snows and frosts of deep winter, the Christmas Rose ventures bravely out into the bleak weather, and with modest and serene courage holds her own against its powers. The snow lying over it keeps it from freezing; and if one brushes away this beautiful covering, the Christmas Rose appears with its lovely, white, gold-centred blossoms, laughing at the frost. It blooms steadily on until it can say 'Good day' to spring's first blossom – the little snowdrop. And so, through all the year, there are flowers blooming in our dear northern land, Denmark.

Thus it was that Nina escaped the witch, who, being a forest witch, did not know of the Christmas Rose, because it is a garden flower.

1916

FATHER CHRISTMAS

Karl Ove Knausgaard

Yesterday evening I was standing on a gravel road, it was drizzling, I was dressed in a red coat, on my feet I wore long woolen stockings over my best shoes, and on my head I wore a mask which seemed to stare up into the damp and compact darkness of the sky. In one hand I held a jute sack, in the other an old-fashioned lantern. As I approached the lit-up house at the end of the road, I stopped, opened the lantern, lit the tea light, closed the little hatch, pulled the mask down over my face, slung the sack over my shoulder, bent my back, and walked with the short steps of an old man over to the window.

Up until now I had felt a little nervous, but the nervousness disappeared the moment I bent over, it was as if I had become an old man and was no longer playing the part. I rapped on the window. There was the sound of running steps from within, and I drew back a little. A child's face was pressed against the windowpane. I lifted my hand in trembling greeting and continued over to the entrance door, which shortly after was flung open. Merry Christmas to all, I said in a piping voice. The boy stared at me intensely for a few seconds, clearly prepared to expose me, before he rather anxiously withdrew. His parents appeared, they looked smilingly at me and asked whether I wanted something to fortify myself. I shook my head. I'm driving, I said, looking at the boy. What is your name, then? I asked. He said his name. I repeated it, mumbling to myself as I rummaged through the sack. When I handed him his present, he tore off the wrapping in an explosion of movement. Shortly after I was standing outside again, by the short wall of the house, with the mask pulled up over my head and a glowing cigarette in my mouth.

The father came out, peering around him. Over here! I said in a low voice. Well, that went pretty well, he said, stopping in front of me. Yes, I said. It seems he fell for it this year too. Can I bum one off you? the father asked. Sure, I said. We walked along the road to my car, which was parked at the end of it, at the crossroads where the main road went by. We got in. Smart move to park here, the father said. He was sure he was going to find you out because of the car. Yes, I said, and drove into the country-side. The road was completely deserted, even as it passed through the village, there wasn't a person in sight. I parked near the school, and we got out into the rain. Would you like a whisky? I asked. He nodded, and I got out the glasses and the bottle I had in the car, poured us drinks. It was unusually quiet; on any other evening a car would have passed occasionally. When our glasses were empty, I put mine back in the car, took off my coat and handed it to him. He stuck one arm into the sleeve, took the whisky glass in his other hand and stuck his other arm in. The coattails flapped in the wind. I handed him the mask. So you'll be along in a couple of minutes then, I said and started toward the house. Two of the children came out when they heard the door open. They had refused to believe that I had really gone out to buy ciga-rettes, so I held the pack out to them as proof.

I'm not Father Christmas, and I've been to the gas station to buy cigarettes, just like I said, I said. They didn't know quite what to believe. Just then there was a knock on the door. Who can it be? I said. The older child gave me an ironic look. I opened the door, and there was Father Christmas with the lantern in his hand and the sack over his shoulder. Are there any good children here? he said.

He didn't have a piping voice, but spoke with a Finland-Swedish accent. Mum, Mum, Father Christmas is here! the youngest shouted. The others at the party came out, and the hall filled with people. We stood in a semicircle staring at Father Christmas, who rummaged slowly through his sack and pulled out presents one by one, handing them solemnly to the children, who stared at him as if in a daze. Would you like something to fortify yourself? I asked, and he nodded, downing the glass of cognac in one go.

After he left, the children were far too engrossed in the presents to notice that I went out after him. He was standing by the car waiting for me, still wearing the mask.

It struck me how sinister he looked, in those familiar surroundings, with the grotesque mask covering his face.

I took out the bottle again and poured two drinks, handing him one.

Well, merry Christmas, he said, raising his glass. Merry Christmas, I said.

2015

THE LITTLE MATCH GIRL

Hans Christian Andersen

It was dreadfully cold; it was snowing fast, and was almost dark, as evening came on – the last evening of the year. In the cold and the darkness, there went along the street a poor little girl, bareheaded and with naked feet. When she left home she had slippers on, it is true; but they were much too large for her feet – slippers that her mother had used till then, and the poor little girl lost them in running across the street when two carriages were passing terribly fast. When she looked for them, one was not to be found, and a boy seized the other and ran away with it, saying he would use it for a cradle someday, when he had children of his own.

So on the little girl went with her bare feet that were red and blue with cold. In an old apron that she wore were bundles of matches, and she carried a bundle also in her hand. No one had bought so much as a bunch all the long day, and no one had given her even a penny.

Poor little girl! Shivering with cold and hunger she crept along, a perfect picture of misery.

The snowflakes fell on her long flaxen hair, which hung in pretty curls about her throat; but she thought not of her beauty nor of the cold. Lights gleamed in every window, and there came to her the savoury smell of roast goose, for it was New Year's Eve. And it was this of which she thought.

In a corner formed by two houses, one of which projected beyond the other, she sat cowering down. She had drawn under her little feet, but still she grew colder and colder; yet she dared not go home, for she had sold no matches and could not bring a penny of money. Her father would certainly beat her; and, besides, it was cold enough at home, for they had only the roof above them, and though the largest holes had been stopped with straw and rags, there were left many through which the cold wind could whistle.

And now her little hands were nearly frozen with cold. Alas! A single match might do her good if she might only draw it from the bundle, rub it against the wall, and warm her fingers by it. So at last she drew one out. *Whisht!*

How it blazed and burned! It gave out a warm, bright flame like a little candle, as she held her hands over it. A wonderful little light it was. It really seemed to the little girl as if she sat before a great iron stove with polished brass feet and brass shovel and tongs. So blessedly it burned that the little maiden stretched out her feet to warm them also. How comfortable she was! But lo! The flame went out, the stove vanished, and nothing remained but the little burned match in her hand.

She rubbed another match against the wall. It burned brightly, and where the light fell upon the wall it became transparent like a veil, so that she could see through it into the room. A snow-white cloth was spread upon the table, on which was a beautiful china dinner service, while a roast goose, stuffed with apples and prunes, steamed famously and sent forth a most savoury smell. And what was more delightful still, and wonderful, the goose jumped from the dish, with knife and fork still in its breast, and waddled along the floor straight to the little girl.

But the match went out then, and nothing was left to her but the thick, damp wall.

She lighted another match. And now she was under a most beautiful Christmas tree, larger and far more prettily trimmed than the one she had seen through the glass doors at the rich merchant's. Hundreds of wax tapers were burning on the green branches, and gay figures, such as she had seen in shop windows, looked down upon her. The child stretched out her hands to them; then the match went out.

Still the lights of the Christmas tree rose higher and higher. She saw them now as stars in heaven, and one of them fell, forming a long trail of fire.

'Now someone is dying,' murmured the child softly; for her grandmother, the only person who had loved her, and who was now dead, had told her that whenever a star falls a soul mounts up to God.

She struck yet another match against the wall, and again it was light; and in the brightness there appeared before her the dear old grandmother, bright and radiant, yet sweet and mild, and happy as she had never looked on Earth.

'Oh, grandmother,' cried the child, 'take me with you. I know you will go away when the match burns out. You, too, will vanish, like the warm stove, the splendid New Year's feast, the beautiful Christmas tree.' And lest her grandmother should disappear, she rubbed the whole bundle of matches against the wall.

And the matches burned with such a brilliant light that it became brighter than noonday. Her grandmother had never looked so grand and beautiful. She took the little girl in her arms, and both flew together, joyously and gloriously, mounting higher and higher, far above the earth; and for them there was neither hunger, nor cold, nor care – they were with God.

But in the corner, at the dawn of day, sat the poor girl, leaning against the wall, with red cheeks and smiling mouth – frozen to death on the last evening of the old year. Stiff and cold she sat, with the matches, one bundle of which was burned.

'She wanted to warm herself, poor little thing,' people said. No one imagined what sweet visions she had had, or how gloriously she had gone with her grandmother to enter upon the joys of a new year.

1845

THE LEGEND OF THE CHRISTMAS ROSE

Selma Lagerlöf

R obber Mother, who lived in Robbers' Cave in Göinge Forest, went down to the village one day on a begging tour. Robber Father, who was an outlawed man, did not dare to leave the forest, but had to content himself with lying in wait for the wayfarers who ventured within its borders. But at that time travellers were not very plentiful in southern Skåne. If it so happened that the man had had a few weeks of ill luck with his hunt, his wife would take to the road. She took with her five youngsters, and each youngster wore a ragged leathern suit and birch bark shoes and bore a sack on his back as long as himself. When Robber Mother stepped inside the door of a cabin, no one dared refuse to give her whatever she demanded; for she was not above coming back the following night and setting fire to the house if she had not been well received. Robber Mother and her brood were worse than a pack of wolves, and many a man felt like running a spear through them; but it was never done, because they all knew that the man stayed up in the forest, and he would have known how to wreak vengeance if anything had happened to the children or the old woman.

Now that Robber Mother went from house to house and begged, she came one day to Övid, which at that time was a cloister. She rang the bell of the cloister gate and asked for food. The watchman let down a small wicket in the gate and handed her six round bread cakes – one for herself and one for each of the five children.

While the mother was standing quietly at the gate, her youngsters were running about. And now one of them came and pulled at her skirt, as a signal that he had discovered something which she ought to come and see, and Robber Mother followed him promptly.

The entire cloister was surrounded by a high and strong wall, but the youngster had managed to find a little back gate which stood ajar. When Robber Mother got there, she pushed the gate open and walked inside without asking leave, as it was her custom to do.

Övid Cloister was managed at that time by Abbot Hans, who knew all about herbs. Just within the cloister wall he had planted a little herb garden, and it was into this that the old woman had forced her way.

At first glance Robber Mother was so astonished that she paused at the gate. It was high summer, and Abbot Hans's garden was so full of flowers that the eyes were fairly dazzled by the blues, reds and yellows as one looked into it. But presently an indulgent smile spread over her features, and she started to walk up a narrow path that lay between many flower beds.

In the garden a lay brother walked about, pulling up weeds. It was he who had left the door in the wall open, that he might throw the weeds and tares on the rubbish heap outside.

When he saw Robber Mother coming in, with all five youngsters in tow, he ran toward her at once and ordered them away. But the beggar woman walked right on as before. She cast her eyes up and down, looking now at the stiff white lilies which spread near the ground, then on the ivy climbing high upon the cloister wall, and took no notice whatever of the lay brother.

He thought she had not understood him, and wanted to take her by the arm and turn her toward the gate. But when the robber woman saw his purpose, she gave him a look that sent him reeling backward. She had been walking with back bent under her beggar's pack, but now she straightened herself to her full height. 'I am Robber Mother from Göinge Forest; so touch me if you dare!' And it was obvious that she was as certain she would be left in peace as if she had announced that she was the Queen of Denmark.

And yet the lay brother dared to oppose her, although now, when he knew who she was, he spoke reasonably to her, 'You must know, Robber Mother, that this is a monks' cloister, and no woman in the land is allowed within these walls. If you do not go away, the monks will be angry with me because I forgot to close the gate, and perhaps they will drive me away from the cloister and the herb garden.'

But such prayers were wasted on Robber Mother. She walked straight ahead among the little flower beds and looked at the hyssop with its magenta blossoms, and at the honeysuckles, which were full of deep orange-coloured flower clusters.

Then the lay brother knew of no other remedy than to run into the cloister and call for help.

He returned with two stalwart monks, and Robber Mother saw that now they meant business! With feet firmly planted she stood in the path and began shrieking in strident tones all the awful vengeance she would wreak on the cloister if she couldn't remain in the herb garden as long as she wished. But the monks did not see why they need fear her and thought only of driving her out. Then Robber Mother let out a perfect volley of shrieks, and, throwing herself upon the monks, clawed and bit at them; so did all the youngsters. The men soon learned that she could overpower them, and all they could do was to go back into the cloister for reinforcements.

As they ran through the passageway which led to the cloister, they met Abbot Hans, who came rushing out to learn what all this noise was about. Then they had to confess that Robber Mother from Göinge Forest had come into the cloister and that they were unable to drive her out and must call for assistance.

But Abbot Hans upbraided them for using force and forbade their calling for help. He sent both monks back to their work, and although he was an old and fragile man, he took with him only the lay brother.

When Abbot Hans came out in the garden, Robber Mother was still wandering among the flower beds. He regarded her with astonishment. He was certain that Robber Mother had never before seen an herb garden; yet she sauntered leisurely among all the small patches, each of which had been planted with its own species of rare flower, and looked at them as if they were old acquaintances. At some she smiled, at others she shook her head.

Abbot Hans loved his herb garden as much as it was possible for him to love anything earthly and perishable. Wild and terrible as the old woman looked, he couldn't help liking that she had fought with three monks for the privilege of viewing the garden in peace. He came up to her and asked in a mild tone if the garden pleased her.

Robber Mother turned defiantly toward Abbot Hans, for she expected only to be trapped and overpowered. But when she noticed his white hair and bent form, she answered peaceably, 'First, when I saw this, I thought I had never seen a prettier garden; but now I see that it can't be compared with one I know of.'

Abbot Hans had certainly expected a different answer. When he heard that Robber Mother had seen a garden more beautiful than his, a faint flush spread over his withered cheek. The lay brother, who was standing close by, immediately began to censure the old woman. 'This is Abbot Hans,' said he, 'who with much care and diligence has gathered the flowers from far and near for his herb garden. We all know that there is not a more beautiful garden to be found in all Skåne, and it is not befitting that you, who live in the wild forest all the year around, should find fault with his work.'

'I don't wish to make myself the judge of either him or you,' said Robber Mother. 'I'm only saying that if you could see the garden of which I am thinking you would uproot all the flowers planted here and cast them away like weeds.'

But the Abbot's assistant was hardly less proud of the flowers than the Abbot himself, and after hearing her remarks he laughed derisively. 'I can understand that you only talk like this to tease us. It must be a pretty garden that you have made for yourself amongst the pines in Göinge Forest! I'd be willing to wager my soul's salvation that you have never before been within the walls of an herb garden.'

Robber Mother grew crimson with rage to think that her word was doubted, and she cried out: 'It may be true that until today I had never been within the walls of an herb garden; but you monks, who are holy men, certainly must know that on every Christmas Eve the great Göinge Forest is transformed into a beautiful garden, to commem-orate the hour of our Lord's birth. We who live in the forest have seen this happen every year. And in that garden I have seen flowers so lovely that I dared not lift my hand to pluck them.'

The lay brother wanted to continue the argument, but Abbot Hans gave him a sign to be silent. For, ever since his childhood, Abbot Hans had heard it said that on every

Christmas Eve the forest was dressed in holiday glory. He had often longed to see it, but he had never had the good fortune. Eagerly he begged and implored Robber Mother that he might come up to the Robbers' Cave on Christmas Eve. If she would send only one of her children to show him the way, he could ride up there alone, and he would never betray them – on the contrary, he would reward them, in so far as it lay in his power.

Robber Mother said no at first, for she was thinking of Robber Father and of the peril which might befall him should she permit Abbot Hans to ride up to their cave. At the same time the desire to prove to the monk that the garden which she knew was more beautiful than his got the better of her, and she gave in. 'But more than one follower you cannot take with you,' said she, 'and you are not to waylay us or trap us, as sure as you are a holy man.'

This Abbot Hans promised, and then Robber Mother went her way. Abbot Hans commanded the lay brother not to reveal to a soul that which had been agreed upon. He feared that the monks, should they learn of his purpose, would not allow a man of his years to go up to the Robbers' Cave.

Nor did he himself intend to reveal his project to another human being. And then it happened that Archbishop Absalon from Lund came to Övid and remained through the night. When Abbot Hans was showing him the herb garden, he got to thinking of Robber Mother's visit, and the lay brother, who was at work in the garden, heard Abbot Hans telling the bishop about Robber Father, who these many years had lived as an outlaw in the forest, and asking him for a letter of ransom for the man, that he might lead an honest life among respectable folk. 'As things are now,' said Abbot Hans, 'his children are growing up into worse malefactors than himself, and you will soon have a whole gang of robbers to deal with up there in the forest.'

But the Archbishop replied that he did not care to let the robber loose among honest folk in the villages. It would be best for all that he remain in the forest.

Then Abbot Hans grew zealous and told the Bishop all about Göinge Forest, which, every year at Yuletide, clothed itself in summer bloom around the Robbers' Cave. 'If these bandits are not so bad but that God's glories can be made manifest to them, surely we cannot be too wicked to experience the same blessing.'

The Archbishop knew how to answer Abbot Hans. 'This much I will promise you, Abbot Hans,' he said, smiling, 'that any day you send me a blossom from the garden in Göinge Forest, I will give you letters of ransom for all the outlaws you may choose to plead for.'

The lay brother apprehended that Bishop Absalon
believed as little in this story of Robber Mother's as he
himself; but Abbot Hans perceived nothing of the sort,
but thanked Absalon for his good promise and said that
he would surely send him the flower.

Abbot Hans had his way. And the following Christmas
Eve he did not sit at home with his monks in Övid
Cloister, but was on his way to Göinge Forest. One of
Robber Mother's wild youngsters ran ahead of him, and
close behind him was the lay brother who had talked with
Robber Mother in the herb garden.

Abbot Hans had been longing to make this journey, and
he was very happy now that it had come to pass. But it
was a different matter with the lay brother who accompanied him. Abbot Hans was very dear to him, and he
would not willingly have allowed another to attend him
and watch over him; but he didn't believe that he should
see any Christmas Eve garden. He thought the whole thing
a snare which Robber Mother had, with great cunning,
laid for Abbot Hans, that he might fall into her husband's
clutches.

While Abbot Hans was riding toward the forest, he saw
that everywhere they were preparing to celebrate Christmas.
In every peasant settlement fires were lighted in the bath-
house to warm it for the afternoon bathing. Great hunks

of meat and bread were being carried from the larders into the cabins, and from the barns came the men with big sheaves of straw to be strewn over the floors.

As he rode by the little country churches, he observed that each parson, with his sexton, was busily engaged in decorating his church; and when he came to the road which leads to Bösjo Cloister, he observed that all the poor of the parish were coming with armfuls of bread and long candles, which they had received at the cloister gate.

When Abbot Hans saw all these Christmas preparations, his haste increased. He was thinking of the festivities that awaited him, which were greater than any the others would be privileged to enjoy.

But the lay brother whined and fretted when he saw how they were preparing to celebrate Christmas in every humble cottage. He grew more and more anxious, and begged and implored Abbot Hans to turn back and not to throw himself deliberately into the robber's hands.

Abbot Hans went straight ahead, paying no heed to his lamentations. He left the plain behind him and came up into desolate and wild forest regions. Here the road was bad, almost like a stony and burr-strewn path, with neither bridge nor plank to help them over brooklet and rivulet. The farther they rode, the colder it grew, and after a while they came upon snow-covered ground.

It turned out to be a long and hazardous ride through the forest. They climbed steep and slippery side paths, crawled over swamp and marsh, and pushed through windfall and bramble. Just as daylight was waning, the robber boy guided them across a forest meadow, skirted by tall, naked leaf trees and green fir trees. At the back of the meadow loomed a mountain wall, and in this wall they saw a door of thick boards. Now Abbot Hans understood that they had arrived, and dismounted. The child opened the heavy door for him, and he looked into a poor mountain grotto, with bare stone walls. Robber Mother was seated before a log fire that burned in the middle of the floor. Alongside the walls were beds of virgin pine and moss, and on one of these beds lay Robber Father asleep.

'Come in, you out there!' shouted Robber Mother without rising, 'and fetch the horses in with you, so they won't be destroyed by the night cold.'

Abbot Hans walked boldly into the cave, and the lay brother followed. Here were wretchedness and poverty! And nothing was done to celebrate Christmas. Robber Mother had neither brewed nor baked; she had neither washed nor scoured. The youngsters were lying on the floor around a kettle, eating; but no better food was provided for them than a watery gruel.

Robber Mother spoke in a tone as haughty and dicta-torial as any well-to-do peasant woman. 'Sit down by the fire and warm yourself, Abbot Hans,' said she, 'and if you have food with you, eat, for the food which we in the forest prepare you wouldn't care to taste. And if you are tired after the long journey, you can lie down on one of these beds to sleep. You needn't be afraid of over-sleeping, for I'm sitting here by the fire keeping watch. I shall awaken you in time to see that which you have come up here to see.'

Abbot Hans obeyed Robber Mother and brought forth his food sack; but he was so fatigued after the journey he was hardly able to eat, and as soon as he could stretch himself on the bed, he fell asleep.

The lay brother was also assigned a bed to rest upon, but he didn't dare sleep, as he thought he had better keep his eye on Robber Father to prevent his getting up and capturing Abbot Hans. But gradually fatigue got the better of him, too, and he dropped into a doze.

When he woke up, he saw that Abbot Hans had left his bed and was sitting by the fire talking with Robber Mother. The outlawed robber sat also by the fire. He was a tall, raw-boned man with a dull, sluggish appearance. His back was turned to Abbot Hans, as though he would have it appear that he was not listening to the conversation.

Abbot Hans was telling Robber Mother all about the Christmas preparations he had seen on the journey, reminding her of Christmas feasts and games which she must have known in her youth, when she lived at peace with mankind. 'I'm sorry for your children, who can never run on the village street in holiday dress or tumble in the Christmas straw,' said he.

At first Robber Mother answered in short, gruff sentences, but by degrees she became more subdued and listened more intently. Suddenly Robber Father turned toward Abbot Hans and shook his clenched fist in his face. 'You miserable monk! Did you come here to coax from me my wife and children? Don't you know that I am an outlaw and may not leave the forest?'

Abbot Hans looked him fearlessly in the eyes. 'It is my purpose to get a letter of ransom for you from Archbishop Absalon,' said he. He had hardly finished speaking when the robber and his wife burst out laughing. They knew well enough the kind of mercy a forest robber could expect from Bishop Absalon!

'Oh, if I get a letter of ransom from Absalon,' said Robber Father, 'then I'll promise you that never again will I steal so much as a goose.'

The lay brother was annoyed with the robber folk for daring to laugh at Abbot Hans, but on his own account he was well pleased. He had seldom seen the Abbot sitting more peaceful and meek with his monks at Övid than he now sat with these wild robber folk.

Suddenly Robber Mother rose. 'You sit here and talk, Abbot Hans,' she said, 'so that we are forgetting to look at the forest. Now I can hear, even in this cave, how the Christmas bells are ringing.'

The words were barely uttered when they all sprang up and rushed out. But in the forest it was still dark night and bleak winter. The only thing they marked was a distant clang borne on a light south wind.

'How can this bell ringing ever awaken the dead forest?' thought Abbot Hans. For now, as he stood out in the winter darkness, he thought it far more impossible that a summer garden could spring up here than it had seemed to him before.

When the bells had been ringing a few moments, a sudden illumination penetrated the forest; the next moment it was dark again, and then the light came back. It pushed its way forward between the stark trees, like a shimmering mist. This much it effected: the darkness merged into a faint daybreak. Then Abbot Hans saw that the snow had vanished from the ground, as if someone had removed a carpet, and the earth began to take on a green covering. Then the ferns shot up their fronds, rolled like a bishop's staff. The heather that grew on the stony hills and the bog-myrtle rooted in the ground moss dressed themselves quickly in new bloom. The moss tufts thickened and raised themselves, and the spring blossoms shot upward their swelling buds, which already had a touch of colour.

Abbot Hans's heart beat fast as he marked the first signs of the forest's awakening. 'Old man that I am, shall I behold such a miracle?' thought he, and the tears wanted to spring to his eyes. Again it grew so hazy that he feared the darkness would once more cover the earth; but almost immediately there came a new wave of light. It brought with it the splash of rivulet and the rush of cataract. Then the leaves of the trees burst into bloom, as if a swarm of green butterflies came flying and clustered on the branches. It was not only trees and plants that awoke, but crossbill finches hopped from branch to branch, and the woodpeckers hammered on the limbs until the splinters fairly flew around them. A flock of starlings from upcountry lighted in a fir top to rest. They were paradise starlings. The tips of each tiny feather shone in brilliant reds, and, as the birds moved, they glittered like so many jewels.

Again, all was dark for an instant, but soon there came a new light wave. A fresh, warm south wind blew and scattered over the forest meadow all the little seeds that had been brought from southern lands by birds and ships and winds, and which could not thrive elsewhere because of this country's cruel cold. These took root and sprang up the instant they touched the ground.

When the next warm wind came along, the blueberries and lingonberries ripened. Cranes and wild geese shrieked in the air, the bullfinches built nests, and the baby squirrels began playing on the branches of the trees.

Everything came so fast now that Abbot Hans could not stop to reflect on how immeasurably great was the miracle that was taking place. He had time only to use his eyes and ears. The next light wave that came rushing in brought with it the scent of newly plowed acres, and far off in the distance the milkmaids were heard coaxing the cows — and the tinkle of the sheep's bells. Pine and spruce trees were so thickly clothed with red cones that they shone like crimson mantles. The juniper berries changed colour every second, and forest flowers covered the ground till it was all red, blue, and yellow.

Abbot Hans bent down to the earth and broke off a wild strawberry blossom, and, as he straightened up, the berry ripened in his hand.

The mother fox came out of her lair with a big litter of black-legged young. She went up to Robber Mother and scratched at her skirt, and Robber Mother bent down to her and praised her young. The horned owl, who had just begun his night chase, was astonished at the light and went back to his ravine to perch for the night. The male cuckoo crowed, and his mate stole up to the nests of the little birds with her egg in her mouth.

Robber Mother's youngsters let out perfect shrieks of delight. They stuffed themselves with wild strawberries that hung on the bushes, large as pinecones. One of them played with a litter of young hares; another ran a race with some young crows, which had hopped from their nest before they were really ready; a third caught up an adder from the ground and wound it around his neck and arm.

Robber Father was standing out on a marsh eating raspberries. When he glanced up, a big black bear stood beside him. Robber Father broke off an osier twig and struck the bear on the nose. 'Keep to your own ground, you!' he said. 'This is my turf.' Then the huge bear turned around and lumbered off in another direction.

New waves of warmth and light kept coming, and now they brought with them seeds from the starflower. Golden pollen from rye fields fairly flew in the air. Then came butterflies, so big that they looked like flying lilies. The beehive in a hollow oak was already so full of honey that it dripped down on the trunk of the tree. Then all the flowers whose seed had been brought from foreign lands began to blossom. The loveliest roses climbed up the mountain wall in a race with the blackberry vines, and from the forest meadow sprang flowers as large as human faces.

Abbot Hans thought of the flower he was to pluck for Bishop Absalon; but each new flower that appeared was more beautiful than the others, and he wanted to choose the most beautiful of all.

Wave upon wave kept coming until the air was so filled with light that it glittered. All the life and beauty and joy of summer smiled on Abbot Hans. He felt that earth could bring no greater happiness than that which welled up about him, and he said to himself, 'I do not know what new beauties the next wave that comes can bring with it.'

But the light kept streaming in, and now it seemed to Abbot Hans that it carried with it something from an infinite distance. He felt a celestial atmosphere enfolding him, and tremblingly he began to anticipate, now that Earth's joys had come, that the glories of heaven were approaching.

Then Abbot Hans marked how all grew still; the birds hushed their songs, the flowers ceased growing, and the young foxes played no more. The glory now nearing was such that the heart wanted to stop beating; the eyes wept without one's knowing it; the soul longed to soar away into the Eternal. From far in the distance faint harp tones were heard, and celestial song, like a soft murmur, reached him.

Abbot Hans clasped his hands and dropped to his knees. His face was radiant with bliss. Never had he dreamed that even in this life it should be granted him to taste the joys of heaven, and to hear angels sing Christmas carols!

But beside Abbot Hans stood the lay brother who had accompanied him. In his mind there were dark thoughts. 'This cannot be a true miracle,' he thought, 'since it is revealed to malefactors. This does not come from God, but has its origin in witchcraft and is sent hither by Satan. It is the Evil One's power that is tempting us and compelling us to see that which has no real existence.'

From afar were heard the sound of angel harps and the tones of a Miserere. But the lay brother thought it was the evil spirits of hell coming closer. 'They would enchant and seduce us,' sighed he, 'and we shall be sold into perdition.'

The angel throng was so near now that Abbot Hans saw their bright forms through the forest branches. The lay brother saw them, too; but at the back of all this wondrous beauty he saw only some dread evil. For him it was the devil who performed these wonders on the anniversary of our Saviour's birth. It was done simply for the purpose of more effectually deluding poor human beings.

All the while the birds had been circling around the head of Abbot Hans, and they let him take them in his hands. But all the animals were afraid of the lay brother; no bird perched on his shoulder, no snake played at his feet. Then there came a little forest dove. When she marked that the angels were nearing, she plucked up courage and flew down on the lay brother's shoulder and laid her head against his cheek.

Then it appeared to him as if sorcery were come right upon him, to tempt and corrupt him. He struck with his hand at the forest dove and cried in such a loud voice that it rang throughout the forest, 'Go thou back to hell, whence thou art come!'

Just then the angels were so near that Abbot Hans felt the feathery touch of their great wings, and he bowed down to earth in reverent greeting.

But when the lay brother's words sounded, their song was hushed and the holy guests turned in flight. At the same time the light and the mild warmth vanished in unspeakable terror for the darkness and cold in a human heart. Darkness sank over the earth, like a coverlet; frost came, all the growths shriveled up; the animals and birds hastened away; the rushing of streams was hushed; the leaves dropped from the trees, rustling like rain.

Abbot Hans felt how his heart, which had but lately swelled with bliss, was now contracting with insufferable agony. 'I can never outlive this,' thought he, 'that the angels from heaven had been so close to me and were driven away; that they wanted to sing Christmas carols for me and were driven to flight.'

Then he remembered the flower he had promised Bishop Absalon, and at the last moment he fumbled among the leaves and moss to try to find a blossom. But he sensed how the ground under his fingers froze and how the white snow came gliding over the ground. Then his heart caused him even greater anguish. He could not rise, but fell prostrate on the ground and lay there.

When the robber folk and the lay brother had groped their way back to the cave, they missed Abbot Hans. They took brands with them and went out to search for him. They found him dead upon the coverlet of snow.

Then the lay brother began weeping and lamenting, for he understood that it was he who had killed Abbot Hans because he had dashed from him the cup of happiness which he had been thirsting to drain to its last drop.

When Abbot Hans had been carried down to Övid, those who took charge of the dead saw that he held his right hand locked tight around something which he must have grasped at the moment of death. When they finally got his hand opened, they found that the thing which he had held in such an iron grip was a pair of white root bulbs, which he had torn from among the moss and leaves.

When the lay brother who had accompanied Abbot Hans saw the bulbs, he took them and planted them in Abbot Hans's herb garden.

He guarded them the whole year to see if any flower would spring from them. But in vain he waited through the spring, the summer, and the autumn. Finally, when winter had set in and all the leaves and the flowers were dead, he ceased caring for them.

But when Christmas Eve came again, he was so strongly reminded of Abbot Hans that he wandered out into the garden to think of him. And look! As he came to the spot where he had planted the bare root bulbs, he saw that from them had sprung flourishing green stalks, which bore beautiful flowers with silver white leaves.

He called out all the monks at Övid, and when they saw that this plant bloomed on Christmas Eve, when all the other growths were as if dead, they understood that this flower had in truth been plucked by Abbot Hans from the Christmas garden in Göinge Forest. Then the lay brother asked the monks if he might take a few blossoms to Bishop Absalon.

And when he appeared before Bishop Absalon, he gave him the flowers and said: 'Abbot Hans sends you these.

They are the flowers he promised to pick for you from the garden in Göinge Forest.'

When Bishop Absalon beheld the flowers, which had sprung from the earth in darkest winter, and heard the words, he turned as pale as if he had met a ghost. He sat in silence a moment; thereupon he said, 'Abbot Hans has faithfully kept his word and I shall also keep mine.' And he ordered that a letter of ransom be drawn up for the wild robber who was outlawed and had been forced to live in the forest ever since his youth.

He handed the letter to the lay brother, who departed at once for the Robbers' Cave. When he stepped in there on Christmas Day, the robber came toward him with axe uplifted. 'I'd like to hack you monks into bits, as many as you are!' said he. 'It must be your fault that Göinge Forest did not last night dress itself in Christmas bloom.'

'The fault is mine alone,' said the lay brother, 'and I will gladly die for it; but first I must deliver a message from Abbot Hans.' And he drew forth the Bishop's letter and told the man that he was free. 'Hereafter you and your children shall play in the Christmas straw and celebrate your Christmas among people, just as Abbot Hans wished to have it,' said he.

Then Robber Father stood there pale and speechless, but Robber Mother said in his name, 'Abbot Hans has indeed kept his word, and Robber Father will keep his.'

When the robber and his wife left the cave, the lay brother moved in and lived all alone in the forest, in constant meditation and prayer that his hard-heartedness might be forgiven him.

But Göinge Forest never again celebrated the hour of our Saviour's birth; and of all its glory, there lives today only the plant which Abbot Hans had plucked. It has been named the Christmas Rose. And each year at Christmastime she sends forth from the earth her green stalks and white blossoms, as if she never could forget that she had once grown in the great Christmas garden at Göinge Forest.

1908

THE BIRD CATCHERS

Hans Aanrud

It is the morning before Christmas with crackling cold and a sun like a large red disc sunk deep in the frost mist to the south. The valley is still dark and lies gray and cold under a smoke yellow fog, but the light is creeping down the steep, snow-covered sides of the mountain; the mist is melting, and overhead the sky is quite clear – the highest spruce tops in the horizon are touched with a faint, golden streak of sunlight.

Down there in the fog people are bustling about in last minute preparations for the holidays. On every path there are hurrying figures; at every yard the sound of chopping comes from the woodblock or the shed, as the Christmas fuel is piled up; huge baskets of hay are carried from hayloft to stable, and the sheaf for the birds – the best the granary affords – is raised on its pole. In front of the church the sexton is clearing a wider path than usual to the main door, and on the road a solitary sleigh bell tinkles where the doctor is driving homeward.

High above the church, in the shadow of the forest, lies a crofter's low hut, almost hidden under the snow, its walls thickly bearded with frost, the light from a fire of dry twigs shooting up through the broad chimney. Two boys of thirteen or thereabouts are coming out of the door, sturdy little fellows, with their pointed caps pulled down to their eyebrows, their mittens pulled up, and their snow socks buttoned tightly around their knickerbockers.

They are the two mighty and inseparable hunters, Per of the farmhouse and Christian whose home is the crofter's hut.

For a moment they stand still, and the eyes of both follow the road as it winds in a sinuous, slanting line upward along the fences until it is lost in a black hole in the forest.

'It isn't going to be a good day for birds,' says Per, 'it's too clear overhead.'

'Well, it doesn't matter today,' Christian replies.

'No, it doesn't matter.'

They pass by the side of the house; each takes a pair of skis standing there by the wall, lays them across his shoulder and adjusts the staff slantwise under them.

'I suppose we'd better go for the grouse snares first.'

'Yes, and the hare traps. Let's go up through the Lie pasture.'

They hunted birds together, Per and Christian, and bird catchers have their own special duty to perform on Christmas Eve. They were not out for an ordinary tour of inspection of their snares, and so were not keyed to the usual pitch of expectancy. On any other day they would have been sure of finding birds, though as a matter of fact they did not very often get anything; all they had ever caught was one white grouse and one heath cock, but that was only because birds were so awfully scarce this year, for there were not many bird catchers who could beat them at setting snares. Those intended for the grouse were hidden in the finest birch twigs, perfect thickets of them stretching for long distances; and in front of the enclosures meant to entice the larger birds the ground was swept as clean as the best room at home and garnished with fresh juniper that covered the snow far and wide. The hare traps were so dainty that the hare must at least have worn spectacles to see them. So it was natural enough that under ordinary circumstances they expected to find at the very least a wood grouse or its mate at the beginning of their rounds, and they never quite lost hope of getting anyway a heath hen or a hazel grouse before they had passed the last thicket. The birds would have to come down into the forest some time!

But the trip today was altogether different, for they were out to take down their snares, large and small. At Christmas there must be peace even in the forest. Christmas brings peace to birds and running animals. Not a single snare must be set; even the sharp, brightly gleaming fox trap, they knew, had to bite a stick instead of a fox's foot. And this was to last till the day after New Year's. To be sure, there were people who did not set their snares again till after Twelfth Day, but there ought to be some sense in everything; on New Year's Day the Yuletide was over, and it was nothing but papistical superstition about Twelfth Night Kari making her Christmas rounds at Twelfth Tide – so the schoolmaster had told them.

That was the reason why Per and Christian were plodding up through the pasture. It was steep, and they did not make much headway.

Hmm! Either that cap was mighty warm or else there was a change in the weather. At the edge of the forest Per stopped, pulled up his cap, and turned to look back: 'Seems to me it smells like a thaw.'

Christian lifted from his scarf a nose blue with cold. 'It always smells like a thaw in this hill, seems to me, but I guess a fellow can get along without mittens now.' He pulled off his mittens and stuffed them into his pocket.

They stood still a moment and looked down into the valley, where the frost mist still hung heavy. They could barely see the dark, slate-covered steeple of the church looking very long and thin where it rose from the mist. Daylight was steadily gaining ground on the shady side of the mountain, but after a while it turned into a woolly gray: the golden streak of sun along the top paled slowly; the sky lost its bright blue and sank heavily down to the spruce tops which seemed almost to pierce it.

Yes, the weather was turning.

'I think it's going to be a good day for birds after all.'

'That would be just our luck – now we've got to take the snares down.'

'Well, there's nothing to be done about that.'

'No, there's no help for it. If the birds do come down, though, maybe one or two of 'em will stay round till after New Year's, but it's a shame!'

They turned and presently had disappeared in the dark hole between the trees.

The forest was strangely dim and silent and bereft of life. Nothing living in sight – no trace of anything living. Even the squirrels lay still in their moss lined nests, and the wood mice snuggled deep in their holes. Not a breath of wind stirred in the spruce standing stiff and stark under the frozen snow. Not a sound was heard except the soft, measured crunching under their feet. Involuntarily they began to step still more cautiously and cast timid glances into the dim vaults that opened under the branches of the trees.

This lasted a long time; it seemed as though the forest would never end. They drew a breath of relief when the trees parted above them and they could see the Lie pasture ahead. There they put on their skis and went in through the gate.

Here were signs of life in plenty – deep tracks where the hare had criss-crossed over the meadow and circled every bush. But now the footprints were almost obliterated by melting and frost, and there were no new marks; even the hare was probably shivering under the thickest brush.

Well, then it didn't matter so much about taking down the hare traps.

First they went to the hayloft, where they had a double trap right in the door, and fastened up the noose carefully so as to leave the passage free. Now the hare could run in and out as much as he pleased. From there they went along the fence – they had a trap at every fence post – and did the same.

Let all go free at Christmas!

On they went straight across the high pasture to the edge of the mountain tarn, where low willows grew. There they had prepared enclosures for the grouse; almost invisible they were with every twig covered by thick, furry frost. It was not worthwhile to take them all apart – just a poke here and there with the ski staff was enough to make them collapse and the nooses drop down so that no grouse could possibly get his head into them. They walked along the thicket twice to make sure that not a single clump of brush was forgotten. No, everything was all right, and at that they started to go back the way they had come, down toward the edge of the forest.

They were headed for the big bird snares.

The silence no longer seemed so oppressive; they were getting used to it and no longer jumped whenever a mass of snow slid down from the branches of a spruce as they passed.

The sky was getting darker; the woolly gray colour had spread all over it, and now and then a large, loose flake of snow came slowly sailing down through the air, but the fog had lifted – yes, the weather was turning. They hardly noticed it, for they were walking quickly, winding in and out among the spruce, in the direction of the part of the forest where the snares were set. They had no thought for anything except that the snares had to come down. Shouting and laughing, they leaped down the steepest places, tumbled and were buried in the drift, sprang up, shaking the heaviest snow from their caps, then pressed on again like snow men in the woods. Today there was no reason why they should be quiet.

Now there was only one enclosure left, the large one out on the knoll where they could look out over the valley. Usually they would take a roundabout way, but today they headed straight down.

Suddenly there was a loud rustling in the trees. A great blackbird flew up, circled out over the knoll on widespread wings against a gray sky, swung around again and swept back into the forest, leaving a broad black wake where it brushed the snow from the branches.

Both boys stood stock-still, almost crouching, their faces pale and tense, their eyes following the flight of the bird and staring at the point where it had vanished. Then they started as from a trance, looked at each other, but did not speak for a few moments. Involuntarily their eyes turned again to the black track through the forest.

When Per tried to speak, he drew in his breath till he almost choked on the words. 'The devil!'

'It must have been a wood grouse.'

'If we'd come a minute sooner we might have caught it.'

'Maybe it's broken the noose!'

They crept forward. All the tense caution of the woods had come over them again, and they advanced as stealthily as if there had been a bird in every bush. Ah, there were the tracks, like huge paws in the snow; there it had settled, had walked right up to the snare, but had flown up, apparently frightened, just at the moment when it was going to go in. The noose hung round and perfect – they surely had been near to catching it.

In their vexation they looked up at the sky and for the first time noticed that it was beginning to snow. So now it was going to be just the right kind of weather; now the big birds would come down.

'Isn't that the darndest – ' Per's voice was trembling.

'That fellow will come back all right now he's got a taste of the juniper,' said Christian.

'He sure will, and he won't wait longer than till tomorrow either.'

'There isn't a finer place in all the forest.'

They discussed the matter from every angle, went over the tracks again, beat the snow down from the nearest branches as if by accident, and shook the pine and juniper twigs in the thicket till they stood fresh and green; angrily they tore off a few handfuls of juniper needles and threw them, as if in spite, in the direction of the snare. The juniper needles looked very green and inviting as they lay there on the white snow.

After a few minutes of this, they paused, and looked down over the valley, where the thickly falling snow drifted down in light, feathery masses. Both were silent as though each were waiting for the other to say something.

Finally Per spoke. 'Well, I suppose we'd better get started.'

Christian looked at him uncertainly. 'Ye-es, I suppose we'd better. Do you want to go first?'

'No, you can go first.'

Christian still lingered as though waiting for something; then he dug his staff deep down in the snow, took a start, and slid rapidly down the hill.

Per waited a moment and stood looking back over his shoulder at the bird thicket. Ah, Christian was out of sight already; he had better get started too.

That last snare they forgot to take down.

'Strange how quiet Per is today,' said his mother in the afternoon. 'Is anything the matter, Per?'

No, nothing was the matter.

Per went about looking pale and dejected; he could not settle down to anything, but glanced at the weather every few minutes.

It was getting milder, and the snow fell evenly and thickly. Now and then Per would start for his skis, but each time he put them back to the wall again.

At last, while the others were at their dinner, he seemed to take a sudden resolve. Noiselessly he took down his skis, fastened them to his feet, and started across the field. When he had got behind the fence where he could not be seen from the house, he turned up the mountain. It was too steep for skis, so he took them off and, holding one in each hand, used them as paddles; in this way he crawled up the mountain, leaving a deep track in the loose snow behind him. When he had gained the level of the crofter's hut, he stopped and peeped over the fence.

He wondered if Christian had gone out; his skis were not in their usual place by the wall. Perhaps he had gone down to get something at the store. In that case Per could have spared himself this roundabout way. But it might be that Christian had taken his skis in only to bend them. It was just as well to be on the safe side and keep to the way where he could not be seen from the window.

And Per plodded on behind the fence and did not turn into the road until he was far above the level of the crofter's place.

What the deuce – who could have passed here now? There were tracks in the road as if someone had walked dragging his skis after him. Well, it was no concern of Per's; he would have to hurry.

He fastened his skis on his feet again and went through the forest, as fast as he could in the new-fallen snow, straight for the knoll where they had seen the big black-bird.

It was quite dark before he came so near that he could see the thickets where the snares were.

Per stopped and held his breath – there was something black moving over there. For a moment he was frightened, until he caught sight of a ski staff standing straight up and down in the snow.

He approached cautiously. There was Christian kneeling in the snow, his mittens lying on the snow beside him, while he was busy taking down the snare.

'Is that you, Christian?'

Christian jumped up and stared at him. 'Why, is that you, Per? How you scared me!'

Both stood looking rather sheepish. At last Christian said, 'I got to thinking that we'd forgotten to take down this snare.

'That's just what I got to thinking of. But now you've done it, I see.'

'Yes, it's all fixed.' Christian put on his skis. 'It certainly is snowing.'

'Yes, and it's getting dark too. We'd better get started.'

They stood ready to begin the downward trip.

Suddenly they felt a faint vibration in the air. It seemed as though a broad path had opened through the thickly falling snow; it was as though a stream of light were moving upward on this path, and with it came from afar the heavy clang of a bell that rose and fell.

They took off their caps.

'Now they're ringing in Christmas,' said Christian.

'Yes,' said Per. 'Say, I guess we'll leave the snares down till after Twelfth Day.' With that they slid down the mountainside.

1919

THE BRAVE TIN SOLDIER

Hans Christian Andersen

There were once five-and-twenty tin soldiers, who were all brothers, for they had been made out of the same old tin spoon. They shouldered arms and looked straight before them, and wore a splendid uniform, red and blue. The first thing in the world they ever heard were the words, 'Tin soldiers!' uttered by a little boy, who clapped his hands with delight when the lid of the box in which they lay was taken off. They were given to him for a birthday present, and he stood at the table to set them up. The soldiers were all exactly alike, except one who had only one leg; he had been left to the last, and then there was not enough of the melted tin to finish him, so they made him to stand firmly on one leg, and this caused him to be very remarkable.

The table on which the tin soldiers stood was covered with other playthings, but the most attractive to the eye was a pretty little paper castle. Through the small windows the rooms could be seen. In front of the castle a number of little trees surrounded a piece of looking glass, which was intended to represent a transparent lake. Swans, made of wax, swam on the lake, and were reflected in it. All this was very pretty, but the prettiest of all was a tiny little lady, who stood at the open door of the castle; she, also, was made of paper, and she wore a dress of clear muslin, with a narrow blue ribbon over her shoulders just like a scarf. In front of these was fixed a glittering tinsel rose, as large as her whole face.

The little lady was a dancer, and she stretched out both her arms, and raised one of her legs so high, that the tin soldier could not see it at all, and he thought that she, like himself, had only one leg. 'That is the wife for me,' he thought; 'but she is too grand, and lives in a castle, while I have only a box to live in, five-and-twenty of us altogether, that is no place for her. Still I must try and make her acquaintance.' Then he laid himself at full length on the table behind a snuffbox that stood upon it, so that he could peep at the little delicate lady, who continued to stand on one leg without losing her balance.

When evening came, the other tin soldiers were all placed in the box, and the people of the house went to bed. Then the playthings began to have their own games together, to pay visits, to have sham fights, and to give balls. The tin soldiers rattled in their box; they wanted to get out and join the amusements, but they could not open the lid. The nutcrackers played at leapfrog, and the pencil jumped about the table. There was such a noise that the canary woke up and began to talk, and in poetry too. Only the tin soldier and the dancer remained in their places. She stood on tiptoe, with her legs stretched out, as firmly as he did on his one leg. He never took his eyes from her for even a moment. The clock struck twelve, and, with a bounce, up sprang the lid of the snuffbox; but, instead of snuff, there jumped up a little black goblin, for the snuffbox was a toy puzzle.

'Tin soldier,' said the goblin, 'don't wish for what does not belong to you.'

But the tin soldier pretended not to hear.

'Very well; wait till tomorrow, then,' said the goblin.

When the children came in the next morning, they placed the tin soldier in the window. Now, whether it was the goblin who did it, or a draft of wind, is not known, but the window flew open, and out fell the tin soldier, heels over head, from the third story, into the street beneath. It was a terrible fall; for he came head downward, his helmet and his bayonet stuck in between the flagstones, and his one leg up in the air. The housemaid and the little boy went downstairs directly to look for him; but he was nowhere to be seen, although once they nearly trod upon him. If he had called out, 'Here I am,' it would have been all right, but he was too proud to cry out for help while he wore a uniform.

Presently it began to rain, and the drops fell faster and faster, till there was a heavy shower. When it was over, two boys happened to pass by, and one of them said, 'Look, there is a tin soldier. He ought to have a boat to sail in.'

So they made a boat out of a newspaper, and placed the tin soldier in it, and sent him sailing down the gutter, while the two boys ran by the side of it, and clapped their hands. Good gracious, what large waves arose in that gutter! And how fast the stream rolled on! For the rain had been very heavy. The paper boat rocked up and down, and turned itself around sometimes so quickly that the tin soldier trembled; yet he remained firm; his countenance did not change; he looked straight before him, and shouldered his musket. Suddenly the boat shot under a bridge that formed a part of a drain, and then it was as dark as the tin soldier's box.

'Where am I going now?' thought he. 'This is the black goblin's fault, I am sure. Ah, well, if the little lady were only here with me in the boat, I should not care for any darkness.'

Suddenly there appeared a great water rat, who lived in the drain.

'Have you a passport?' asked the rat, 'give it to me at once.' But the tin soldier remained silent and held his musket tighter than ever. The boat sailed on and the rat followed it. How he did gnash his teeth and cry out to the bits of wood and straw, 'Stop him, stop him; he has not paid the toll, and has not shown his pass.' But the stream rushed on stronger and stronger. The tin soldier could already see daylight shining where the arch ended. Then he heard a roaring sound quite terrible enough to frighten the bravest man.

At the end of the tunnel the drain fell into a large canal over a steep place, which made it as dangerous for him as a waterfall would be to us. He was too close to it to stop, so the boat rushed on, and the poor tin soldier could only hold himself as stiffly as possible, without moving an eyelid, to show that he was not afraid. The boat whirled around three or four times, and then filled with water to the very edge; nothing could save it from sinking. He now stood up to his neck in water, while deeper and deeper sank the boat, and the paper became soft and loose with the wet, till at last the water closed over the soldier's head. He thought of the elegant little dancer whom he should never see again, and the words of the song sounded in his ears:

'Farewell, warrior! Ever brave,
Drifting onward to thy grave.'

Then the paper boat fell to pieces, and the soldier sank into the water and immediately afterward was swallowed up by a great fish. Oh how dark it was inside the fish! A great deal darker than in the tunnel, and narrower too, but the tin soldier continued firm, and lay at full length shouldering his musket. The fish swam to and fro, making the most wonderful movements, but at last he became quite still. After a while, a flash of lightning seemed to pass through him, and then the daylight approached, and a voice cried out, 'I declare here is the tin soldier.'

The fish had been caught, taken to the market and sold to the cook, who took him into the kitchen and cut him open with a large knife. She picked up the soldier and held him by the waist between her finger and thumb, and carried him into the room. They were all anxious to see this wonderful soldier who had travelled about inside a fish; but he was not at all proud. They placed him on the table, and – how many curious things do happen in the world! – there he was in the very same room from the window of which he had fallen, there were the same children, the same playthings standing on the table, and the pretty castle with the elegant little dancer at the door. She still balanced herself on one leg and held up the other, so she was as firm as he. It touched the tin soldier so much to see her that he almost wept tin tears, but he kept them back.

He only looked at her and they both remained silent. Presently one of the little boys took up the tin soldier, and threw him into the stove. He had no reason for doing so, therefore it must have been the fault of the black goblin who lived in the snuffbox. The flames lighted up the tin soldier, as he stood, the heat was very terrible, but whether it proceeded from the real fire or from the fire of love he could not tell. Then he could see that the bright colours were faded from his uniform, but whether they had been washed off during his journey or from the effects of his sorrow, no one could say. He looked at the little lady, and she looked at him. He felt himself melting away, but he still remained firm with his gun on his shoulder.

Suddenly the door of the room flew open and the draught of air caught up the little dancer; she fluttered like a sylph right into the stove by the side of the tin soldier, and was instantly in flames and was gone. The tin soldier melted down into a lump, and the next morning, when the housemaid took the ashes out of the stove, she found him in the shape of a little tin heart. But of the little dancer nothing remained but the tinsel rose, which was burned black as a cinder.

1838

THE HOLY NIGHT

Selma Lagerlöf

When I was five years old I had such a great sorrow! I hardly know if I have had a greater since then.

It was then that my grandmother died. Up to that time, she used to sit every day on the corner sofa in her room and tell stories.

I remember Grandmother told story after story from morning till night, and we children sat beside her, quite still, and listened. It was a glorious life! No other children had such happy times as we did.

It isn't much that I recollect about my grandmother. I remember that she had very beautiful snow-white hair, and stooped when she walked, and that she always sat and knitted a stocking.

And I even remember that when she had finished a story, she used to lay her hand on my head and say: 'All this is as true, as true as that I see you and you see me.'

I also remember that she could sing songs, but this she did not do every day. One of the songs was about a knight and a sea troll, and had this refrain: 'It blows cold, cold weather at sea.'

Then I remember a little prayer she taught me, and a verse of a hymn.

Of all the stories she told me, I have but a dim and imperfect recollection. Only one of them do I remember so well that I should be able to repeat it. It is a little story about Jesus's birth.

Well, this is nearly all that I can recall about my grandmother, except the thing which I remember best; and that is, the great loneliness when she was gone.

I remember the morning when the corner sofa stood empty and when it was impossible to understand how the days would ever come to an end. That I remember. That I shall never forget!

And I recollect that we children were brought forward to kiss the hand of the dead and that we were afraid to do it. But then someone said to us that it would be the last time we could thank Grandmother for all the pleasure she had given us.

And I remember how the stories and songs were driven from the home-stead, shut up in a long black casket, and how they never came back again.

I remember that something was gone from our lives. It seemed as if the door to a whole beautiful, enchanted world – where before we had been free to go in and out – had been closed. And now there was no one who knew how to open that door.

And I remember that, little by little, we children learned to play with dolls and toys, and to live like other children. And then it seemed as though we no longer missed our grandmother, or remembered her.

But even today – after forty years – as I sit here and gather together the legends about Christ, which I heard out there in the Orient, there awakes within me the little legend of Jesus's birth that my grandmother used to tell, and I feel impelled to tell it once again, and to let it also be included in my collection.

It was Christmas Day and all the folks had driven to church except grandmother and me. I believe we were all alone in the house. We had not been permitted to go along, because one of us was too old and the other was too young. And we were sad, both of us, because we had not been taken to early mass to hear the singing and to see the Christmas candles.

But as we sat there in our loneliness, Grandmother began to tell a story.

There was a man who went out in the dark night to borrow live coals to kindle a fire. He went from hut to hut and knocked. 'Dear friends, help me!' said he. 'My wife has just given birth to a child, and I must make a fire to warm her and the little one.'

But it was way in the night, and all the people were asleep. No one replied. The man walked and walked. At last, he saw the gleam of a fire a long way off. Then he went in that direction and saw that the fire was burning in the open. A lot of sheep were sleeping around the fire, and an old shepherd sat and watched over the flock.

When the man who wanted to borrow fire came up to the sheep, he saw that three big dogs lay asleep at the shepherd's feet. All three awoke when the man approached and opened their great jaws, as though they wanted to bark; but not a sound was heard. The man noticed that the hair on their backs stood up and that their sharp, white teeth glistened in the firelight. They dashed toward him.

He felt that one of them bit at his leg and one at his hand and that one clung to his throat. But their jaws and teeth wouldn't obey them, and the man didn't suffer the least harm.

Now the man wished to go farther, to get what he needed. But the sheep lay back-to-back and so close to one another that he couldn't pass them. Then the man stepped upon their backs and walked over them and up to the fire. And not one of the animals awoke or moved.

When the man had almost reached the fire, the shepherd looked up. He was a surly old man, who was unfriendly and harsh toward human beings. And when he saw the strange man coming, he seized the long, spiked staff, which he always held in his hand when he tended his flock, and threw it at him. The staff came right toward the man, but, before it reached him, it turned off to one side and whizzed past him, far out in the meadow.

Now the man came up to the shepherd and said to him: 'Good man, help me, and lend me a little fire! My wife has just given birth to a child, and I must make a fire to warm her and the little one.'

The shepherd would rather have said no, but when he pondered that the dogs couldn't hurt the man, and the sheep had not run from him and that the staff had not wished to strike him, he was a little afraid, and dared not deny the man that which he asked.

'Take as much as you need!' he said to the man.

But then the fire was nearly burned out. There were no logs or branches left, only a big heap of live coals, and the stranger had neither spade nor shovel wherein he could carry the red-hot coals.

When the shepherd saw this, he said again: 'Take as much as you need!' And he was glad that the man wouldn't be able to take away any coals.

But the man stopped and picked coals from the ashes with his bare hands, and laid them in his mantle. And he didn't burn his hands when he touched them, nor did the coals scorch his mantle; but he carried them away as if they had been nuts or apples.

And when the shepherd, who was such a cruel and hard-hearted man, saw all this, he began to wonder to himself. What kind of a night is this, when the dogs do not bite, the sheep are not scared, the staff does not kill, or the fire scorch? He called the stranger back and said to him: 'What kind of a night is this? And how does it happen that all things show you compassion?'

Then said the man: 'I cannot tell you if you yourself do not see it.' And he wished to go his way, that he might soon make a fire and warm his wife and child.

But the shepherd did not wish to lose sight of the man before he had found out what all this might portend. He got up and followed the man till they came to the place where he lived.

Then the shepherd saw the man didn't have so much as a hut to dwell in, but that his wife and babe were lying in a mountain grotto, where there was nothing except the cold and naked stone walls.

But the shepherd thought that perhaps the poor innocent child might freeze to death there in the grotto; and, although he was a hard man, he was touched, and thought he would like to help it. And he loosened the knapsack from his shoulder, took from it a soft white sheepskin, gave it to the strange man, and said that he should let the child sleep on it.

But just as soon as he showed that he, too, could be merciful, his eyes were opened, and he saw what he had not been able to see before, and heard what he could not have heard before.

He saw that all around him stood a ring of little silver-winged angels, and each held a stringed instrument, and all sang in loud tones that tonight the Saviour was born who should redeem the world from its sins.

Then he understood how all things were so happy this night that they didn't want to do anything wrong.

And it was not only around the shepherd that there were angels, but he saw them everywhere. They sat inside the grotto, they sat outside on the mountain, and they flew under the heavens. They came marching in great companies, and, as they passed, they paused and cast a glance at the child.

There was such jubilation and such gladness and songs and play! And all this he saw in the dark night whereas before he could not have made out anything. He was so happy because his eyes had been opened that he fell upon his knees and thanked God.

What that shepherd saw, we might also see, for the angels fly down from heaven every Christmas Eve, if we could only see them.

You must remember this, for it is as true, as true as that I see you and you see me. It is not revealed by the light of lamps or candles, and it does not depend upon sun and moon, but that which is needful is that we have such eyes as can see God's glory.

1908

CHRISTMAS EVE

Vigdis Hjorth

There is a nervousness accompanying the children's expectations that increases the thirst. I would like to drink from early morning. But that won't do. I mustn't get drunk. If I get drunk, it'll ruin everything; they'll be terrible, the days they are staying with me, cleaning up, tears, impossible. I mustn't get drunk. There's nothing that increases your thirst as much as knowing you mustn't get drunk. I won't be able to make it without drinking, but I mustn't get drunk. I mustn't have a beer after skiing, as I usually do, which is the reason I go skiing; perhaps I'll drop skiing when I can't have a beer afterward. I mustn't get drunk. I mustn't become unsteady. I mustn't laugh, I mustn't sing. I mustn't tell jokes. I mustn't show signs of intoxication. I mustn't make the children feel uncertain about that. I can have a glass of wine for dinner, but I mustn't become drunk. I mustn't talk too loudly. My voice mustn't quiver. I mustn't be in high spirits, then they become suspicious and insecure. I mustn't stay in the cellar too long if I have to go down to the cellar to get fruit for the fruit salad, then they could think that I'm drinking down there, on the sly. I mustn't drink on the sly. I mustn't stagger. I must speak clearly, I must be steady on my feet. They're cooking, they're standing in the kitchen cooking and have opened a beer, my son and my son-in-law. My oldest daughter has taken the car to the gas station convenience store to buy salt. I'm cutting the fruit, I mustn't open a beer. They're watching me, I'm cutting the fruit. They're looking for signs. I have to bear it until the gifts have been handed out. Then I'll go to bed, then I'll light the fire in my own part of the house, and drink red wine and feel safe, alone and unsupervised. I can have one glass of wine for dinner. No more. They keep track. I can't effortlessly reach out for the bottle. The one who's filling the glasses usually forgets my glass. It just happens, or it's agreed upon. I'm allowed two glasses. If I speak clearly, if I don't laugh, if I walk steadily, if I don't drink the first glass too greedily, if I pretend that I have forgotten that there's wine on the table. I'm allowed two glasses if I sip the first one. Then I'm allowed one more toward the end of the meal. The house smells of pork ribs. My son's wearing an apron and is having a beer while he's making sauerkraut from scratch. My son-in-law's making spicy meatballs and is having a beer. I'm the only one who notices. They have no fear of becoming drunk. My son can become quite drunk, but he is son, not mother, he doesn't live with the fear. I hope he becomes drunk. I hope he drinks so much that he becomes drunk and forgets about me. But my youngest daughter doesn't forget. I put a cider in the freezer when I go down to get the pineapple. My youngest daughter calls to say she's on her way. She usually doesn't drink. She has a strained relationship to alcohol. She saves drinking until she's at a party with friends. When she's with us, her family, she doesn't drink. She's damaged. I'm the one who has damaged her. I wish she would drink and become happy and forget me. She comes and studies me, but I haven't been drinking, I haven't had a beer after skiing, because I haven't been skiing. My son asks if she wants a beer. My ears prick up, I hope she says yes, that she drinks many beers and lots of wine and gets drunk and forgets me so I can get drunk. I wish everyone would get drunk and lose themselves in gifts and forget about me. She shakes her head, she doesn't want a beer, that's the damage.

★

I go to get pomegranates in the cellar and take the cider out of the freezer. I drink it as fast as I can, I'm so thirsty. I listen for steps, but there aren't any. I mustn't stay for too long, have to go up soon, I drink and drink. Then it's empty, it helped and gets worse. Now I feel guilty. But I'm not going to get drunk. I can take a lot of cider before I get drunk. I'm not going to get drunk, I'm just going to calm my nerves. They don't understand that. If they knew that I opened a cider and drank it, they'd feel insecure and worry about how the evening would end. It has to be done in secret. I'm going to keep my promise. I'm not going to get drunk. I go up again with the pomegranates and behave as naturally as I can possibly can. Cider doesn't smell. I ask my youngest daughter if she had enjoyed the day with her father yesterday. My voice doesn't tremble, I don't think anyway. I'm listening to myself, am so focused on myself that I have problems talking, moving. I talk and move as little as possible. The cider is warming my blood. I feel the warmth spreading, try to lower my shoulders, but they carry my shame. We had a nice time, she said. They'd eaten catfish. They'd accompanied their meal with a good white wine, I know that, but I don't ask about the wine. Alcohol is not a subject here. She doesn't seem to notice the cider. I hope she'll relax and understand that I won't get drunk, so I can relax. The fruit salad is ready. The pork ribs are ready. My son-in-law is uncorking the red wine he has brought. It goes well with the pork. My oldest daughter calls and asks if she should buy some ice cream as well. The others want that; she'll soon arrive with the ice cream and put it in the freezer where there's a cider. I have to remove it before she comes. I said I'll carry the fruit salad down to the cellar where it'll stay cool. That sounds quite natural. No one asks, no one seems to suspect anything. I cover the salad with plastic wrap, elaborately and slowly as if there's no rush. Carry it down to the cellar, take the cider from the freezer and drink it fast, even if it's not cold. I feel completely clearheaded, even more clear headed, completely calm, calmer, like a hardened criminal during the misdeed. I talk calmly to myself. Calm, now. I go up and set the table, utterly focused. My daughter looks at me, I concentrate on the steps to the drawer and the steps back, the cutlery in the right place, glasses and plates. I don't drop anything, I don't break anything. I don't slur my words, because I don't say anything, I don't stagger. My oldest daughter comes back from the gas station with ice cream and puts it in the freezer. We sit down, finally. My son-in-law fills our glasses. He asks if I'll have a drink. Just one, I say, loudly, to reassure. He fills my glass. Less in mine than in the other glasses, it seems to me, I study him while he's pouring the lovely red wine, how it rises in the glasses, how high in those of the others, how high in mine. My youngest daughter says she doesn't want wine, loudly, to make sure I hear it. She wants soda water. She gets the soda water and puts it down hard on the table. We wish one another merry Christmas and lift our glasses, finally. I keep the wine in my mouth as long as possible. I take small, small sips. They eat, we eat, they eat more than they drink. The bottle is empty, but they have more left in their glasses, so they don't open another one. I look over at the kitchen bench, at the other bottle. Now my son, finally, goes to get it. Opens it and fills his glass and asks if anyone else wants some. I say, as collected as I can, as effortlessly as I can, that I wouldn't mind another glass. The last one, I add, loudly, so everyone can hear it. My son looks at his sister, the youngest one, my son looks at his sister, the oldest one, they don't say anything, they keep their opinions to themselves. My son fills my glass half-full and puts the bottle back on the bench. We're silent. We eat, they eat, I try to let the wine last. Then I get the fruit salad from the cellar without drinking cider, don't dare to. Ice cream and fruit salad, I still have wine in my glass, don't dare to empty it and be without. Lift the glass to my mouth and dip my tongue in the wine. The dessert consumed, shortly there'll be gifts, shortly it'll be over. I get a garbage bag from the cellar for the wrapping paper, drop into my bedroom and spray red wine from a carton into my mouth, it helps, it'll soon be over, it'll be alright, I can endure another hour. I go up and I get gifts. I say thank you, I'm not going to get drunk. My youngest daughter is calmer now. Sees that I don't drink, that I don't stagger, that I don't hold a glass in my hand that I keep lifting to my mouth like other Christmas Eves, when I slowly faded away. Now I'm present, it seems. My whole body, my whole head, everything in me is longing for my room, the fireplace, the bed, the wine. It's soon midnight, it's soon time, I'll give them another half hour. They're relaxed, they laugh, talk, the danger has passed. Mum isn't drunk, she has kept her promise. I'll soon say good night, I say and yawn. It's been a long day, I say and sigh. Pick up some pieces of wrapping paper and put them in the garbage bag, as if I'm thinking of things like that to do, as if there's no rush. I go to the kitchen and put the plates in the dishwasher, empty the glasses and put them in. They're not coming in to check, they're not afraid, everything has gone well. Put the leftovers in the fridge, stick my head into the living room and say it again, time for bed, it's been a long day. Go down to my room and close the door. Sit down on the bed, open the bottle of 200 kroner good wine, which is my reward. Take out my finest glass, fill it, gulp the wine. I didn't get drunk, now I can get drunk. Light the fire, put on clean pajamas, settle down in bed, they're not going to come down, I've gone to bed, I've said good night, they're not going to know what I'm doing. Everything has gone well, now I can drink. My bed has clean sheets, I drink and look at the fireplace and know I have more wine in the locked cupboard. It's over, it's over and done with, I'm on my own, finally, happy.

2015

GIANTS IN THE EARTH

O. E. Rölvaag

The day before Christmas Eve snow fell. It fell all that night and the following forenoon. Still weather, and dry, powdery snow. Murk without, and leaden dusk in the huts. People sat oppressed in the somber gloom.

Things were in a bad way over at Per Hansa's now; everyone knew it and feared what might befall both Beret and him. No one could help; all that could be done was to bide the time, for soon a change must come!

'Listen, folks,' said Tönseten, trying to comfort them as best he could. 'Beret can't keep this up forever! I think you had better go over to her again, Kjersti!'

Both neighbour women were now taking turns at staying with her, each one a day at a time. They saw clearly that Per Hansa was more in need of help than Beret; there was no helping her now, while something, at least, could be done for him and the children. Christmas would soon be here, too, and the house ought to be made comfortable and cosy!

They all felt very sorry for Per Hansa. He walked about like a ragged stray dog; his eyes burned with a hunted look. Each day, the children were sent over to Hans Olsa's to stay for a while; if they remained longer than they had been told, he made no protest; at last they formed the habit of staying the whole day. He did not realise that it was bad for Beret to be without them so much; he tried to keep the talk going himself, but she had little to say; she answered in mono-syllables and had grown peculiarly quiet and distant. In the shadow of a faint smile which she occasionally gave him there lay a melancholy deeper than the dusk of the Arctic Sea on a rainy, gray fall evening.

About noon of Christmas Eve the air suddenly cleared. An invisible fan was pushed in under the thick, heavy curtain that hung trembling between earth and heaven – made a giant sweep, and revealed the open, blue sky overhead. The sun shone down with powerful beams, and started a slight trickling from the eaves. Toward evening, it built a golden fairy castle for itself out yonder, just beyond Indian Hill.

The children were at Hans Olsa's; And-Ongen wanted to stay outside and watch the sunset. Sofie had told her that today was Christmas Eve, and that on every Christmas Jesus came down from heaven. The child asked many questions: Would he come driving? Couldn't they lend him the pony? Sofie hardly thought so – he probably would be driving an angel-pony!

Store-Hans, who was listening to them, thought this very silly and just like girls. He knew better! Toward evening he suddenly wanted to go home, and was almost beside himself when his godfather said that he couldn't: all the children were to stay with Sofie tonight. They had to hold him back by force. This was *Christmas Eve.* He understood very well that something was about to go wrong at home. Why had his mother looked so wan and worn of late, and his father acted so queer that one couldn't talk to him?

That afternoon Beret was in childbed. The grim struggle marked Per Hansa for life; he had fought his way through many a hard fight, but they had all been as nothing compared with this. He had ridden the frail keel of a capsized boat on the Lofoten seas, had seen the huge, combing waves snatch away his comrades one by one, and had rejoiced in the thought that the end would soon come for him also; but things of that sort had been mere

175

child's play. *This* was the uttermost darkness. Here was neither beginning nor end – only an awful void in which he groped alone.

Sörine and Kjersti had both arrived a long time since. When they had come he had put on his coat and gone outside; but he hadn't been able to tear himself many steps away from the house.

Now it was evening; he had wandered into the stable to milk Rosie, forgetting that she had gone dry long ago; he had tended to Injun and the oxen, without knowing what he was about. He listened to Beret wailing in the other room, and his heart shriveled; thus a weak human being could not continue to suffer, and yet live. And this was his own Beret!

He stood in the door of the stable, completely undone. Just then Kjersti ran out to find him; he must come in at once; Beret was asking for him! Kjersti was gone in a flash. He entered the house, took off his outdoor clothes, and washed his hands.

Beret sat half-dressed on the edge of the bed. He looked at her, and thought that he had never seen such terror on any face. God in heaven – this was beyond human endurance!

She was fully rational, and asked the neighbour women to leave the room for a moment, as she had something to say to her husband. She spoke with great composure; they obeyed immediately. When the door closed behind them Beret rose and came over to him, her face distorted. She laid a hand on each of his shoulders, and looked deep into his eyes, then clasped her hands behind his neck and pulled him violently toward her. Putting his arms firmly around her, he lifted her up gently and carried her to the bed; there he laid her down. He started to pull the covers over her. But she held on to him; his solicitous care she heeded not at all.

When he had freed himself, she spoke brokenly, between gasps:

'Tonight I am leaving you. Yes, I must leave you. I know this is the end! The Lord has found me out because of my sins ... It is written, "To fall into the hands of the living God!" ... Oh! – It is terrible! I can't see how you will get along when you are left alone though I have only been a burden to you lately. You had better give And-Ongen to Kjersti. She wants a child so badly – she is a kind woman. You must take the boys with you – and *go away from here!* How lonesome it will be for me to lie here all alone!'

Tears came to her eyes, but she did not weep; between moans she went on strongly and collectedly: 'But promise me one thing: put me away in the big chest! I have emptied it and made it ready. Promise to lay me away in the big chest, Per Hansa! And you must be sure to dig the grave deep! You haven't heard how terribly the wolves howl at night! Promise to take plenty of time and dig deep down – do you hear!'

His wife's request cut Per Hansa's heart like sharp ice; he threw himself on his knees beside the bed and wiped the cold perspiration from her face with a shaking hand.

'There now, blessed Beret-girl of mine!' His words sounded far off – a note of frenzy in them. 'Can't you understand that this will soon be over? Tomorrow you'll be as chipper as a lark again!'

Her terror tore her only the worse. Without heeding his words, she spoke with great force out of the clearness of her vision: 'I shall die tonight. Take the big chest! At first I thought of asking you not to go away when spring came and leave me here alone. But that would be a sin! I tell you, you *must* go! Leave as soon as spring comes! Human beings cannot exist here! They grow into beasts.'

The throes were tearing her so violently now that she could say no more. But when she saw him rise she made a great effort and sat up in bed.

'Oh! – don't leave me! – don't go away! Can't you see how sorely I need you? And now I shall die! Love me – oh, do love me once more, Per Hansa!' She leaned her body toward him. 'You must go back to Norway. Take the children with you ... let them grow up there. Ask father and mother to forgive me! Tell father that I am lying in the big chest! Can't you stay with me tonight, stay with me and love me? Oh! – *there they come for me!'*

Beret gave a long shriek that rent the night. Then she sobbed violently, praying that they should not take her away from Per Hansa.

Per Hansa leaped to his feet, and found his voice.

'Satan – now you shall leave her alone!' he shouted, flinging the door open and calling loudly to the women outside. Then he vanished into the darkness.

No one thought of seeking rest that night. All the evening, lights shone from the four huts; later they were extinguished in two of them; but in the house of Hans Olsa four men sat on, grieving over the way things were going at Per Hansa's. When they could bear the suspense no longer someone proposed going over to get news.

Tönseten offered to go first. When he came back little sense could be gathered from what he said. He had not been allowed inside; the women were in a frenzy; the house was completely upset; Beret was wailing so loud that it was dreadful to hear. And Per Hansa himself was nowhere to be found. 'We must go and look for him, boys! Haven't you got a Bible or something to read from, Hans Olsa? This is an awful thing!'

There they sat, each occupied with his own thoughts – but all their thoughts were of the same trend. If Beret died tonight, it would go hard with Per Hansa – indeed it would. In that case he probably wouldn't stay out here very long. But if he went away, the rest of them might as well pack up and go, too!

Sam ran over to inquire; then Henry; at last it was Hans Olsa's turn. He managed to get a couple of words with his wife, who said that Beret would hardly stand it. No one had seen Per Hansa.

'Can you imagine where the man can be keeping himself?' asked Tönseten, giving voice to the fear that oppressed them all. 'May the Lord preserve his wits, even if He chooses to take his wife away!'

Per Hansa walked to and fro outside the hut all night long; when he heard someone coming he would run away into the darkness. He could not speak to a living soul tonight. As soon as the visitor had gone he would approach the hut again, circle around it, stop, and listen. Tears were streaming down his face, though he was not aware of it. Every shriek that pierced the wall of the hut drove him off as if a whip had struck him; but as soon as it had died out, something would draw him back again. At intervals he went to the door and held it ajar. What did Per Hansa care for custom and decency, now that his Beret lay struggling with death! Each time Sörine came to the door, each time she shook her head sadly, and told him there was no change yet; it was doubtful if Beret would be able to pull through; no person could endure this much longer; God have mercy on all of them!

That was all the comfort Sörine could give him. Then he would rush off into the darkness again, to continue his endless pacing. When daylight came they found a hard path tramped into the snow around the hut.

The night was well-nigh spent when the wails in there began to weaken – then died out completely, and did not come again. Per Hansa crept up to the door, laid his ear close to it, and listened. So now the end had come! His breath seemed to leave him in a great sob. The whole prairie began to whirl around with him; he staggered forward a few steps and threw himself face downward on the snow.

But then suddenly things didn't seem so bad to him, really not so bad. He saw a rope ... a rope ... It was a good, strong rope that would hold anything. It hung just inside the barn door – and the crossbeam ran just there! No trick at all to find these things. Per Hansa felt almost happy at the thought; that piece of rope was good and strong – and the crossbeam ran just there!

A door opened somewhere; a gleam of light flashed across the snow, and vanished. Someone came out of the hut quietly – then stopped, as if searching.

'Per Hansa!' a low voice called. 'Per Hansa, where are you?' He rose and staggered toward Kjersti like a drunken man.

'You must come in at once!' she whispered, and hurried in before him.

The light was dim in there; nevertheless it blinded him so strongly that he could not see a thing. He stood a moment leaning against the door until his eyes had grown accustomed to it. A snug, cosy warmth enveloped him; it carried with it an odd, pleasant odour. The light, the warmth, and the pleasant smell overcame him like sweet sleep that holds a person who has been roused, but who does not care to awaken just yet.

'How is it?' he heard a man's voice ask. Then he came back to his senses. Was that he himself speaking?

'You'll have to ask Sörrina,' Kjersti answered.

Sörine was tending something on the bed; not until now did he discover her – and wake up completely. What was this? ... the expression on her face? Wasn't it beaming with motherly goodness and kindliness?

'Yes, here's your little fellow! I have done all I know how. Come and look at him. It's the greatest miracle I ever saw, Per Hansa, that you didn't lose your wife tonight, and the child, too! I pray the Lord I never have to suffer so!'

'Is there any hope?' was all Per Hansa could gasp – and then he clenched his teeth.

'It looks so, now – but you had better christen him at once. We had to handle him roughly, let me tell you.'

'*Christen him?*' Per Hansa repeated, unable to comprehend the words.

'Why, yes, of course. I wouldn't wait, if he were mine.'

Per Hansa heard no more – for now Beret turned her head and a wave of such warm joy welled up in him that all the ice melted. He found himself crying softly, sobbing like a child. He approached the bed on tiptoe, bent over it, and gazed down into the weary, pale face. It lay there so white and still; her hair, braided in two thick plaits, flowed over the pillow. All the dread, all the tormenting fear that had so long disfigured her features, had vanished completely. She turned her head a little, barely opened her eyes, and said, wearily:

'Oh, leave me in peace, Per Hansa. Now I was sleeping so well.' The eyelids immediately closed.

Per Hansa stood for a long time looking at his wife, hardly daring to believe what he saw. She slept peacefully;

a small bundle lay beside her, from which peeped out a tiny, red, wrinkled face. As he continued to gaze at her he sensed clearly that this moment was making him a better man!

At last he gathered his wits sufficiently to turn to Sörine and ask: 'Tell me, what sort of a fellow is this you have brought me – a boy or a girl?'

'Heavens! Per Hansa, how silly you talk!' Kjersti and Sörine both had to laugh as they looked at Per Hansa; such a foolish, simple expression they had never seen on the face of a living man! But Sörine immediately grew serious once more, and said that this was no time for joking; the way they had tugged and pulled at him during the night, you couldn't tell what might happen; Per Hansa must get the child christened right away; if he put if off, she refused to be responsible.

A puzzled expression came over the grinning face.

'You'd better do that christening yourself, Sörrina!'

No! – she shook her head emphatically. That wasn't a woman's job – he must understand! 'And you ought to have it done with proper decorum, and thank the Lord for doing so well by you!'

Without another word Per Hansa found his cap and went to the door; but there he paused a moment to say: 'I know only one person around here who is worthy to perform such an act; since you are unwilling, I must go and get him. In the meanwhile, you make ready what we will need; the hymn book you'll find on the shelf over by the window. I won't be long!'

The kindly eyes of Sörine beamed with joy and pride; she knew very well the one he intended to get; this was really handsome of Per Hansa! But then another thought crossed her mind; she followed him out, and closed the door after her.

'Wait a minute,' she said. 'I must tell you that your boy was born with the caul! I think you ought to find a very beautiful name for him!'

'What are you saying, Sörrina!'

'Yes, sir – that he had! And you know what *that* means!'

Per Hansa drew his sleeve across his face – then turned and walked away. A moisture dimmed his eyes – he could not see.

Outside it was now broad daylight; the sun stood some distance up in the sky, looking down on a desolate Earth. It was going to be cold today, Per Hansa noticed; clouds of frosty mist like huge writhing serpents curled over the surface of the purplish-yellow plain. The sunbeams plunging into them kindled a weird light. He tingled with the cold; his eyelashes froze together so that he had to rub them with his mittens to keep them free.

How remarkable – the child had been born with the caul! He quickened his pace; in a moment he was running.

'Peace be upon this house, and a merry Christmas, folks!' he greeted them as he entered Hans Olsa's door. The room was cold; the Solum boys lay in one bed, fully dressed; both were so sound asleep that they did not wake up at his coming. His own children and Sofie lay in the other bed, Ole by himself down at the foot, the other three on the pillow; Store-Hans held And-Ongen close, as if trying to protect her. Hans Olsa and Tönseten had moved their chairs up to the stove, and sat hunched over on either side; Tönseten was nodding, the other was wide awake; both men jumped up when Per Hansa came in, and stood staring at him.

Per Hansa had to laugh outright at them; they were looking at him as if they had seen a ghost. But to the two men his laugh sounded pleasanter than anything they had heard in many a year.

'How are things coming?' asked Tönseten, excitedly, working his shoulders.

'Oh, it might have been worse!'

Hans Olsa grasped his hand: 'Will she pull through?'

'It looks that way.'

Then Tönseten suddenly seemed to realise that it was cold in the room; he began to walk around, beating goose with his arms. 'I'm ready to bet both my horses that it's a boy! I can see it in your face!' he exclaimed, still beating.

'All signs point that way, Syvert! But he's in pretty poor condition, Sörrina tells me. Now look here, Hans Olsa: it's up to you to come over and christen the boy for me!'

Hans Olsa looked terror-stricken at his neighbour. 'You must be crazy, Per Hansa!'

'Nothing of the kind, Hans Olsa. You just get yourself ready. It's all written down in the hymn book – what to say, and how to go about it.'

'No, no – I couldn't think of such a thing!' protested Hans Olsa, all atremble with the feeling of awe that had suddenly taken possession of him. 'A sinner like me!'

Then Per Hansa made a remark that Tönseten thought was extremely well put: 'How you stand with the Lord I don't know. But this I do know: that a better man either on land or sea, He will have to look a long way to find. And it seems to me that He has got to take that, too, into His reckoning!'

But Hans Olsa only stood there in terror. 'You'd better ask Syvert to do it!'

Then Tönseten grew alarmed: 'Don't stand there talking like a fool! We all know that if one of us two is to tackle this job, it must be you, Hans Olsa. There is nothing for you to do but go at once; this business won't stand any dillydallying, let me tell you!'

Hans Olsa gazed straight ahead; his helplessness grew so great that he was funny to look at; but no one thought of laughing, just the same. 'If it only won't be blasphemy!' He finally straggled into his big coat and put on his mittens. Then he turned to Tönseten. 'The book says: "In an extreme emergency a layman may perform this act" – isn't that so?'

'Yes, yes – just so! Whatever else you'll need, is written there, too!'

Through the frosty morning the two men walked silently across the prairie, Per Hansa in the lead. When they had covered half the distance he stopped short and said to his neighbour: 'If it had been a girl, you see, she should have been named Beret – I decided that a long while ago ... But seeing that it's a boy, we'll have to name him Per, you must say Peder, of course! I've thought a good deal about Joseph – he was a pretty fine lad, no doubt. But grandfather's name was Per, and there wasn't a braver, worthier man on that part of the coast; so it'll just have to be Per again this time. But say, now – ' Per Hansa paused a moment, pondering; then he looked up at his neighbour, and his eyes began to gleam. 'The boy must have a second name – so you'd better christen him Peder

Seier, for that means victorious! The last is after your Sörrina. She has done me a greater service this night than I can ever repay! And now the boy is to be named after her!'

Hans Olsa could think of nothing to say in answer to all this. They walked on in silence.

When they came into the room, they stepped across the threshold reverently. An air of Sabbath had descended on the room. The sun shone brightly through the window, spreading a golden luster over the white walls; only along the north wall, where the bed stood, a half shadow lingered. The fire crackled in the stove; the coffeepot was boiling. The table had been spread with a white cover; upon it lay the open hymn book, with the page turned down. Beside the hymn book stood a bowl of water; beside that lay a piece of white cloth. Kjersti was tending the stove, piling the wood in diligently. Sörine sat in the corner, crooning over a tiny bundle; out of the bundle at intervals came faint, wheezy chirrups, like the sounds that rise from a nest of young birds.

An irresistible force drew Per Hansa to the bed. She lay sound asleep. Thank God, that awful look of dread had not come back! He straightened himself up and glanced around the room; never before had he seen anything that looked so beautiful.

Sörine got up, went to the table, and bared a little rosy human head.

'If you are going to be the minister here,' she said, turning to her husband, who had remained standing motionless at the door, 'then you must hurry up and get ready. First of all you must wash your hands.'

The next moment they had all gathered around the table.

'Here's the book. Just read it out as well as you can, and we'll do whatever the book says,' Sörine encouraged her husband. She seemed to have taken charge of the ceremony, and spoke in low, reassuring tones, as if she had done nothing else all her life but attend to such duties; and it was her confidence that gave Hans Olsa the courage he needed. He went up to the table, took the book, and read the ritual in a trembling voice, slowly, with many pauses. And so he christened the child Peder Seier, pronouncing the name clearly. Whereupon he said the Lord's Prayer so beautifully that Kjersti exclaimed she had never heard the like.

'There, now!' said Kjersti with great emphasis. 'I don't believe there is a thing lacking to make this christening perfectly correct! Now the coffee is ready and we're all going to have a cup.'

But Per Hansa was searching over in the corner; at last he produced a bottle. First he treated Sörine; then Kjersti. 'If ever two people have earned something good, you two are it! Come on, now, have another little drop! And hurry up about it, please! Hans Olsa and I feel pretty weak in the knees ourselves!'

After a while both food and drink were served. 'It looks as if we are going to have a *real* Christmas, after all!' said Per Hansa with a laugh, as they sat around the table enjoying their coffee.

1924–25

HANS AANRUD (1863–1953) was a Norwegian author of plays, poetry and stories. He was born into a rural family and many of his stories deal with peasant life, while his later works were more urban in nature.

INGVAR AMBJØRNSEN (1956–) is a prize-winning Norwegian author. His novel *Brødre i blodet* (Blood Brothers) was made into a movie nominated for the 2001 Oscar for best foreign film.

HANS CHRISTIAN ANDERSEN (1805–1875) was a Danish author of thousands of popular tales, many of them haunting stories inspired by folklore and others that were entirely original. Andersen's fairy tale 'The Brave Tin Soldier,' was part of a nineteenth-century wave of literature depicting a child's view of the adult world, including E.T.A. Hoffman's 'Nutcracker and the King of Mice,' adapted into the Tchaikovsky ballet traditionally performed at Christmas time.

PETER CHRISTEN ASBJØRNSEN (1812–1885) was a Norwegian scholar and author who trained as a zoologist.

He collected Norwegian folklore with Jørgen Engebretsen Moe and they jointly published folktales and legends. His portrait appears on the Norwegian fifty crown banknote.

VIGDIS HJORTH (1959–) was born in Oslo and is a popular and controversial author in Norway. Much of her writing is autobiographical. Several of her novels deal with contemporary women's search for identity.

KARL OVE KNAUSGAARD (1968–) is a Norwegian author best known for a six-volume autobiographical novel, *My Struggle*. His work has been widely acclaimed, and he is the founder of a publishing house called Pelikanen.

JOHAN KROHN (1841–1925) was a Danish author. His book *Peter's Christmas*, first published in 1866, is a children's classic.

SELMA LAGERLÖF (1858–1940) became the first female author to win the Nobel Prize for Literature in 1909. A Swede, she worked as a teacher in a girls' secondary school where she honed her storytelling gifts.

O. E. RÖLVAAG (1876–1931) was born on a Norwegian island near the Arctic Circle. He migrated to the United

States in 1896, settling first in South Dakota. His most famous book, *Giants in the Earth*, is a realistic novel about the experience of Scandinavian pioneers in the American Midwest. It was written in Norwegian and translated into English, inspiring an opera that won a 1951 Pulitzer Prize.

HJALMAR SÖDERBERG (1869–1941) was a Swedish novelist, playwright, poet and journalist. His books feature melancholy and lovelorn characters in fin de siècle Stockholm. 'I believe in the lust of the flesh and the incurable isolation of the soul,' remarks a figure in Söderberg's most celebrated novel, *Dr. Glas*.

ZACHRIS TOPELIUS (1818–1898) was a Finnish author who wrote in Swedish. His works, including novels, short stories, lyric poems and the libretto of the first Finnish opera, have become part of Finnish national heritage.

'Another Star'
translated from the Norwegian by May-Brit Akerholt

'Christmas Eve'
translated from the Norwegian by May-Brit Akerholt

'Round the Yule Log'
translated from the Norwegian by H. L. Broekstad

'Father Christmas'
From the essay collection *Winter*
translated from the Norwegian by Ingvild Burkey

'Giants in the Earth'
From *Giants in the Earth*
translated from the Norwegian by Lincoln Colcord and
O. E. Rölvaag

'A Christmas Guest'
translated from the Swedish by Pauline Bancroft Flach

'The Emperor's Vision'
translated from the Swedish by Velma Swanston Howard

'The Holy Night'
translated from the Swedish by Velma Swanston Howard

'The Fur Coat'
translated from the Swedish by Edith and Wärner Oland

'The Brave Tin Soldier'
translated from the Danish by H. B. Paull

'The Fir Tree'
translated from the Danish by H. B. Paull

'The Forest Witch'
translated from the Danish by Emilie Poulsson and
Laura E. Poulsson

'A Legend of Mercy'
translated from the Swedish by Emilie Poulsson and
Laura E. Poulsson

'The Little Match Girl'
translated from the Danish by H. B. Paull

'The Bird Catchers'
translated from the Norwegian, translator unknown

VINTAGE CLASSICS

Vintage launched in the United Kingdom in 1990, and was originally the paperback home for the Random House Group's literary authors. Now, Vintage is comprised of some of London's oldest and most prestigious literary houses, including Chatto & Windus (1855), Hogarth (1917), Jonathan Cape (1921) and Secker & Warburg (1935), alongside the newer or relaunched hardback and paperback imprints: The Bodley Head, Harvill Secker, Yellow Jersey, Square Peg, Vintage Paperbacks and Vintage Classics.

From Angela Carter, Graham Greene and Aldous Huxley to Toni Morrison, Haruki Murakami and Virginia Woolf, Vintage Classics is renowned for publishing some of the greatest writers and thinkers from around the world and across the ages – all complemented by our beautiful, stylish approach to design. Vintage Classics' authors have won many of the world's most revered literary prizes, including the Nobel, the Man Booker, the Prix Goncourt and the Pulitzer, and through their writing they continue to capture imaginations, inspire new perspectives and incite curiosity.

In 2007 Vintage Classics introduced its distinctive red spine design, and in 2012 Vintage Children's Classics was launched to include the much-loved authors of our childhood. Random House joined forces with the Penguin Group in 2013 to become Penguin Random House, making it the largest trade publisher in the United Kingdom.

@vintagebooks

penguin.co.uk/vintage-classics